A Night
of Music

D0945209

Marjorie Sandor

A Night of Music

stories

THE ECCO PRESS
NEW YORK

Copyright © 1989 by Marjorie Sandor
All rights reserved

The Ecco Press
26 West 17th Street
New York, NY 10011
Published simultaneously in Canada by
Penguin Books Canada Ltd., Ontario
Printed in the United States of America
Designed by Jody Hanson
FIRST EDITION

The author gratefully acknowledges the editors of the following
magazines, in which several of these stories have appeared: "Staying
Under," *The Agni Review;* "Icarus Descending," "Victrola," *Antæus;* "A
Night of Music," *Black Warrior Review;* "The Gittel," "Still Life," "The
World Is Full of Virtuosos," *The Georgia Review;* "The Bonbon Man,"
Shenandoah; and "Judgement," *The Yale Review.*

Library of Congress Cataloging-in-Publication Data
Sandor, Marjorie.
    A night of music : stories / Marjorie Sandor.
    —1st ed.   p.   cm.
    Contents: The Gittel—Icarus descending—Victrola—Still life—
The bonbon man—The beautiful Amelia—Judgment—Staying
under—A daughter who sings—The world is full of virtuosos
—A night of music.
    I. Title.
PS3569.A5195N5   1989   813'.54—dc20   89-32597

    ISBN 0-88001-236-6

The text of this book is set in Janson.

To my mother and
to the memory of my father

Contents

The Gittel   3

Icarus Descending   23

Victrola   41

Still Life   55

The Bonbon Man   66

The Beautiful Amelia   85

Judgment   106

Staying Under   120

A Daughter Who Sings   133

The World Is Full of Virtuosos   154

A Night of Music   165

A Night of Music

The Gittel

There is a tradition in our family that once in a while a dreamer is born: an innocent whose confused imagination cannot keep up with the civilized world. This person walks around in a haze of dreams, walking eventually right into the arms of the current executioner, blind as Isaac going up the mountain with his father. Nobody knows who started this story—my mother used to say it was a second-rate scholar out to impress the neighbors—but apparently there are characteristics, traits peculiar to this person, and two hundred years ago people knew a catastrophe was on the way if such a person came into their midst. Once, when I was a little girl, I asked Papa to name the traits. He said he couldn't; they'd been lost. All he knew was that this dreamer, before vanishing, always left behind a dreaming child, and that sometimes he thought he was such a child.

My father was a modest man; he came to Ellis Island with his eyebrows up, and they never came down. Furthermore he was the kind of storyteller who rarely got past the scenic details, since every time he let his imagination go his children had nightmares for a week. I remember: I was eight years old, sitting with him on the kitchen stairs, my bedtime cup of milk between us. My mother was scrubbing a pot with steel wool, making that sound that hurts the smallest bones in the body, and in the parlor the alabaster lamp had been lit for my grandmother Gittel's yahrzeit.

The lamp looked different than it does now. We hadn't converted it yet to electric, and it glowed pale orange behind the alabaster. As a child I could look at it for hours, imagining miniature cities on fire, or ladies in a golden room. It didn't have the long crack you see running down the left side. My daughter Rachel did that when she was ten years old, running like a maniac through the room and tripping over the cord. She won't go near it now; at nineteen she thinks it's her destiny to break it. She's a little careless, it's true, but nothing some responsibility wouldn't cure. I'm waiting for her now— she said she was taking the 4:30 bus from the city. I've been thinking about things, and tonight, after we eat, I'm going to tell her she can have the lamp when she and Daniel move into the new apartment.

So, where was I? With Papa? Yes, he was looking away from me, at the lamp in the parlor.

"We don't really know when she died," he said. "Not the exact date. But sometimes I wonder—what if these dreamers are common, nothing extraordinary, people you have to fight to recognize as a sacrifice, a warning. . . ." He bent lower, opening his mouth to speak again. Something rough and wet scratched my wrist; it was the steel wool, all soapy, in my mother's hand.

"Don't romanticize, Bernard," she said. "It's common knowledge that Gittel was a selfish woman who should have had the good sense to stay single. Sacrifice, my foot."

Sometimes I wish I were more like her and less like my father. No matter how many questions a daughter had, she knew when to talk and when to keep quiet. Before my wedding, young as I was, she didn't tell me anything. "Why frighten a person unnecessarily?" she said later. Papa was different. He couldn't hide anything from me. It's from him we get the insomnia and the bad dreams—he always left his children to finish his stories in their sleep.

"The Gittel," he used to say, as if she were a natural phenomenon. A little beauty at sixteen, she had red-gold hair to her waist, fine features, and tiny feet. Thank God, Rachel inherited her feet and not mine. Lucky girl. Tiny feet, this Gittel, and a good dancer and musician. The red in her hair and the musical sense came from the Hungarian; the rest was German going all the way back to the seventeenth century, when the Shapiros settled illegally in Berlin. By 1920 the family was in a good position: respected by the new Berlin intellectuals. Of course it wasn't really the brains, but the red-gold hair and the fine noses that made them comfortable. You can bet if they'd looked more Semitic they'd have caught on sooner to the general news.

She was eighteen then. Her father, along with a handful of other Jewish scholars, had been granted a professorship at the University of Berlin, and the family was able to establish itself in a brick house on Grunewaldstrasse, with real lace curtains and a baby grand. Being her father's pet, Gittel took whatever she liked from his library shelves, and sometimes sat with him when a colleague came to visit. Soon after her eighteenth birthday, she came into his study to borrow a book— without knocking, just like my Rachel. She had just mastered the art of the entrance, and paused where the light from the alabaster lamp would shine best on her hair.

"Papa," she announced. "Where is the Hoffmann?"

Shapiro was deep in conversation with a slender, bearded visitor whose trousers, according to Gittel's standards, were a little short. "Read something else," said her father. "The Romantics are anti-Semitic."

"Not Hoffmann," cried Gittel.

The visitor turned. He cursed himself for having put on his reading glasses, since at that distance he could not see her face or her eyes. He saw hair lit to the color of his own carefully raised flame roses and a brown merino skirt, very trim at the waist. "You enjoy Hoffmann as well?" he asked, squinting.

His name was Yaakov Levy: thirty-five years old and a scholar from Riga, Latvia. Like Shapiro he was enjoying the new generosity of his government. For the first time in his professional life he had had enough money to take the train to Berlin for a lecture series: Shapiro's on Western Religions. After the lecture and a three-hour discussion in the Romanische Café, he had received an invitation to coffee in the professor's home.

He was delirious, first to stand in Shapiro's study, then to make the acquaintance of his household. And still wearing those ridiculous spectacles, the cheap frames warped from the weight of the lenses. He took off his glasses for the formal introduction. His eyes, which had seemed to Gittel to be unnaturally large behind the lenses, now had a fine, granular brilliance, like her mother's antique blue glass vase. It was his eyes that kept her standing there, and his eyes that made Shapiro think to himself: he can't help but be honorable. It's not in his veins as a possibility, unfaithfulness. She's young, but better to send her with a scholar than watch her run off at twenty with a young gentile going through his mystical phase.

Professor Shapiro is not to be blamed. I can imagine his concern, for Gittel was famous for her lively behavior with students. A young man would come to the house on Grunewaldstrasse, stand in the front hall, and within minutes a figure in petticoats would appear running down the curved staircase, shouting "Mama, Mama, I can't get the buttons in back!" Mrs. Shapiro was no help either, in the long run. She wore her hair in a neat coil, fastened her own innumerable buttons without assistance, and on top of that made bread from scratch. Just like my mother, she wouldn't let her daughter into the kitchen until dinner was safe in the oven. "You're a little girl yet," she'd say. "There's plenty of time to learn." I vowed I'd be different with mine. She would make her bed the minute she started to talk back, and help me in the kitchen whenever it was convenient. I wasn't going to make the same mistake.

Mrs. Shapiro got the message from her husband and invited Levy to stay to supper that evening. That meal nearly cost them a suitor, for despite the intensity of his vision and the shortness of his trousers, Levy had a fondness for table manners, and Gittel's were wretched. She tapped her fingers on the white linen, rearranged her cutlery, and sometimes hummed a phrase of music, as if she were alone in her room. He blushed, torn between embarrassment and desire. She, on her side, glanced at him only long enough to compare his eyes to those of Anselmus, the student-hero of a Hoffmann tale, noting that each time she looked at him, a feverish color stained his cheeks. I know this kind of girl: not happy unless she's in the midst of charming someone into his downfall. Gittel hummed and smiled and asked Levy if, after supper, he would turn the piano music for her.

Levy raised his napkin awkwardly to his lips.

"Go ahead," said Shapiro. "We'll finish our discussion later."

Levy had never before turned pages of music for a lady, young or otherwise, and here Gittel sealed her fate. *Turn,* she said, trying out a low, husky cabaret voice. *Turn.* It was easy to obey such a voice. Levy imagined going on and on, watching her narrow, lightly freckled hands touch the keys and lift under the lamplight. Her fingers trembled a little; his heart swelled under his ribs, wanting to protect. . . . When at last she released him into her father's study, he had forgotten Western Religions and inquired after Gittel's status. Shapiro was standing by his desk, a book in his hand.

"Tell me about Latvia," he said. "Things don't flare up there the way they do here, isn't that so?"

"That's true," said Levy. "The nationals have been very liberal."

Shapiro smiled a small, lopsided smile. "She will be a lovely wife, a delight," he said. "And Latvia is good."

Picture the night Gittel was told of her destiny. They stand in the front parlor, and she turns pale yellow, like a late leaf, and begins looking through her music for something she says she's been missing for a long time. Finally she stops looking and says to Levy: "We will live here, in town?" He takes her hands, surprised at the firmness of the thin fingers, the tautness of the palm. The hands don't tremble now.

"I have a house of my own, and a garden," he says. "In a suburb of Riga."

"Mother," cries Gittel. "*Riga?*"

Mrs. Shapiro ushers her daughter from the parlor. Imagine the sound of their two skirts rustling, and how Levy felt watching them leave the room—the upright mother and the daughter, long fingers gripping her skirt. The two men wait in the parlor like displaced ghosts; Professor Shapiro trying over and over to light his pipe; Levy holding himself perfectly still, blinking and pale as if he'd just stepped out of his study into broad daylight.

When Gittel appeared in the doorway again her back was needle-straight. She stepped up to Levy and held out her hand. "Let me play you something," she said.

"Chopin," muttered her father. "Another anti-Semite."

Levy escorted her to the piano, where she played for him the Sixth Prelude, her favorite. It's a strange piece: half delight, half dirge. They say he wrote it during a night of terrible rains. A messenger came to his door: George Sand and her three children had been killed in a carriage accident. He kept composing, unable to leave the piano bench. He wrote the last notes in the morning, just as there was another knock on the door, and her voice . . .

Mrs. Shapiro did not come back into the parlor until Levy was ready to leave. She was as gracious as ever, a remarkable woman; I know how she felt. I can see her face, almost as fragile as her daughter's, the eyelids only a little pink, only a little. I admire that woman.

The wedding picture is right there—on the mantel. When my Rachel was small, she used to take it down and touch her tongue to the dusty glass.

"Don't do that," I'd say.

She'd look at me, already the archaeologist, and say, "I'm cleaning it off for you."

Somewhere in her teens she lost interest; she could walk by that picture without even a glance. I can't do that. I walk past and there's Gittel in the dress her mother made for her by hand: a creamy, flounced thing. Her waist is unbelievable. She's tiny, but then the bridegroom is no giant himself. Great mustaches hide his lips, and he's not wearing his glasses. Without them his eyes appear pale and wide awake, as if when the shutter came down he saw something astonishing. I don't know anything about his childhood or bachelor circumstances; why he should have such eyes on his wedding day I can only attribute to foresight. He was like Shapiro that way. So much foresight he couldn't enjoy the wedding cake.

Beside him the Gittel is serious too; only on her, seriousness doesn't look so sweet. Her lips are set tight together, and her pupils are so dilated that her green eyes look black as caves. Rachel used to look at those eyes.

"I don't like her," she'd say. Somehow even a child knows it's not the usual bridal worry that's in Gittel's eyes. Ten years old, holding that picture in her hand. "Mom," she says to me. "Do I have to leave home like her if I'm bad?"

She gave me a nice shock. When had I ever spoken of Gittel leaving home at eighteen? I played innocent. "Who told you that, Rachel?" I asked.

"You talk in your sleep," she said.

She made me nervous then, she makes me nervous now. At the time, I thought: what good will it do to tell a ten-year-old that when the time comes, she'll be good and ready to leave home?

"You're not a Gittel," I said. "Nobody is going to make you leave home. We just want you to be happy."

She bit her lower lip and big terrible tears dropped on her T-shirt.

"Rachel, you're breaking my heart," I said. "What's the matter?"

"It's okay," she said. "I'll go and pack."

Thank God that phase is over—although with Rachel it's hard to tell. Last month when we looked at that picture together she laughed.

"I used to have nightmares about her," she said.

I acted nonchalant. "Like what?"

"I don't remember. Big melodramas, everybody in the world disappearing—"

"Go on," I said.

Then she gave me such a look. "Mom," she said. "All kids have dreams like that."

"About the end of the world?" I asked.

"Yes."

Sometimes she hurts me with her quick answers. Every family has its stories, why should she deny hers? Besides, she traps me. She was all eagerness: "Mother, what finally happened to Gittel?"

What am I supposed to do? If I start to tell it, and she's in a modern mood, she cuts me off. If she's not, she gets all dreamy on me. Naturally I start thinking about her and Daniel and their archaeology studies, and so I say to her, "Rache, tell me honestly what you plan on doing with those old pots? Read the newspapers, look around you!" I raised her to read the newspapers so nothing should take her by surprise, and she winds up in the ancient ruins. Last week on the phone she said to me: "Mother. I read the newspapers and so does Daniel," and I knew she was biting her lip. It's a bad habit. "I'm coming this weekend," she said, "so you and I can have a talk." I made up my mind right then and there that I wouldn't mention Gittel unless she promises not to interrupt . . .

Gittel bore her husband seven sons in ten years. Papa was number four, Gittel's favorite because he had his father's eyes and could listen to her at the piano without speaking or tugging on her skirt every three minutes. Sometimes she would stop playing and say to him: "Shut your eyes, Bernard, and imagine that this is a baby grand instead of an upright, and that across from us is a maroon divan, where grandpapa sits reading, his glasses slipping down his nose." Other times she took him into the courtyard and lifted her fine nose into the air. "Smell," she said. "Today it smells exactly like April at home." He listened to her describe where the alabaster lamp had stood in the other house (she had it next to the piano in

Riga) and how her mother had given it to her, along with the brass candlesticks, the five handmade lace doilies, and her own key ring to wear at her waist. "A good housekeeper is never without her keys," her mother had said, knowing everything in advance.

Once a week a letter arrived from Grunewaldstrasse, and the family gathered in the parlor to hear Gittel read it. Papa remembered later how his father leaned against the mantel listening carefully to letters that seemed to be about nothing but the weather and fifteenth-century religion. His mother's hands trembled as she read—her voice, too—and sometimes afterward he heard them talking in their bedroom, their voices soft to begin with, then rising, rising.

Gittel captured the little suburb. For months after her departure people talked of how the young mother would be stirring soup in the kitchen and suddenly remember a dream she'd had the night before. Off she'd run to the neighbor's house, bursting in: "Tzipporah, I forgot to tell you what I dreamed about your boy!" Her friends seemed to love this, especially the burning of the soup that went hand in hand with the piece of news, the almost forgotten dream, the stories about Grunewaldstrasse. It was rare in that time and place to find a woman for whom dreams and stories came before soup, and a miracle that, given her dizzy mind and her husband's library heart, any of the seven boys grew up. "Luck," Papa would say to me if Mother was in the room. "Destiny," he'd say if she wasn't.

He was five years old when his father died. Diabetes: that's where Papa got it, and now I have to be careful too. Gittel was twenty-eight, and after the seven boys she still had her figure and her lovely hair. Papa's memory of her is of a woman in a new black silk dress and fine shoes, hushing a baby. It was at his father's funeral that he began to be afraid of her.

The service was held on a little rise in the Jewish cemetery outside Riga. It was a fine March day, the kind of day when the tips of the grass look caught on fire, and gulls go slanting across the sky as if they can't get their balance. The kind of day where you want to run in one direction and then turn and see the figures of people you've left behind, tiny and unreal as paper dolls. Papa wanted to break out of the circle of mourners and run across the knolls and valleys of the cemetery, all the way down to the shore, where the Gulf of Riga stretched endlessly away.

"Come here, Bernard," said Gittel. "Stand in front of me."

She placed one hand lightly on his shoulder, but every time he shifted his weight, her fingers tightened. His brothers stood all around him: Johan, the eldest, almost ten and already a tall boy; Aaron and Yaakov beside him. Pressed tight to their mother's skirt were the two young ones, whose names Papa later forgot, and on her hip, the baby. She stood absolutely still, while around her Levy's friends and relatives rocked back and forth. Papa turned once and looked up at her face. Her narrow jaw was marble white, and her eyes, clear and unreddened, were trained on a tuft of grass blowing beside the open pit. People whispered: "Poor thing, she's in shock. He was everything to her." Only Papa, watching the dark pupils, knew that she was not thinking about her husband. When the rabbi closed his book, Gittel sighed and bent down to Bernard.

"Very soon," she said, "we can go back."

"Back to the house?" said Bernard.

"No," she replied. "Grunewaldstrasse."

For five years no one but Papa knew Gittel's mind. They thought she would pull herself together and become a good manager with all the help she was offered by her women friends. Everybody should be so fortunate; Levy's cousins in the city came by often to take the boys out for a drive, and ladies were always bringing hot dishes by. "With seven boys she must be desperate," they said. The neighbors began to wonder, though, how with seven wild boys they would be hearing Chopin and Mozart four hours together in the morning. Certain shopkeepers began to talk. The dishes stopped coming, and the cousins, after a lecture or two, stopped coming to get the boys. "Let her suffer like other human beings," they said. "A lesson is what she needs."

Maybe by that time it was too late for lessons. I suppose she tried. She worked in her husband's garden, coming up with small, deformed carrots and the smallest heads of cabbage imaginable. She sent the three eldest boys to serve one-year apprenticeships in town, and when they came home for the Sabbath they brought her things from the city, and part of their wages. Bernard she sent to school: Bernard, who wanted nothing more than to be a carpenter like his big brother Johan, whom he worshiped for his muscles and his talk of America. Every day after school Bernard went to the carpenter's house to drink tea with Johan, and every day Johan showed him the tin with the money in it. "They say you can't keep kosher there," he'd say. "But otherwise it's paradise."

Home in the evenings, Bernard let his mother caress his

face. "You have the eyes of your father, and the brains of mine," she'd say. "He is a great teacher in Berlin, and so will you be, when we go home."

"We are home," he'd say, looking at his feet.

"No," she said. "You wait and see."

Gittel's looks were beginning to go. Her hair was no longer that burnished gold color, although the ladies told her she could fix it easily with a little lemon juice and a walk in the sunlight. But Gittel wasn't listening. She played loud, crashing pieces by Chopin and Liszt, and sent Bernard to do all her errands in town so she wouldn't have to face the helpful remarks of the shopkeepers. When he left for school she sent him with letters to mail to Grunewaldstrasse, which came back marked *wrong address.*

One day a letter came from the Shapiros—with another address, in a district of Berlin Bernard had never heard his mother mention. In the morning, he waited beside her writing table while she finished a letter. Over her shoulder he read: *I don't care if it's smaller, we're coming. People stare at me in the street.*

"I'll be back in a minute, Mama," he said. Upstairs in his room he packed a school satchel and hid it in his closet. He would know when she began to pack up her lamp and her candlesticks.

That night Gittel went to the carpenter's house and wept at his table. "We're running out of money," she said. "Can you keep Johan for another year?" The carpenter was surprised; he knew Gittel's people in Germany were well off, that she could get money any time she wanted. He told people later that his first reaction was to refuse: "Lie in your own bed," he wanted to say, but she looked almost ill. Her lovely skin seemed blue, as if she were turning to ice inside. "All right," he said.

Two days later the shoemaker received a visit, and under the pressure of her tears, offered to keep Aaron for a second year. "He works like the devil," he said later, "better than my own sons, and doesn't waste his money." But telling the story, he shook his head: "It's a terrible thing to see a woman trying to give away her children."

The third boy, Yaakov, was finally taken by the Levy cousins, though not until they had given Gittel a piece of their minds. Now that Levy had passed on, they revered him like a saint. "If our Yaakov were alive, what would he say to all this?" "If your Yaakov were alive," she answered, "would any of this be happening?" She was gaunt and smoky-eyed as a gypsy, and sometimes, in the two weeks that followed, she looked at Bernard with such passion that he ran out of the house and took a streetcar to Johan's, where he stayed till suppertime. Late one night, as he was working in his copybook for school, she knelt beside him.

"Bernard," she said. "Are you still having your special dreams?"

He hadn't been able to remember his dreams for weeks. Instead he heard voices all talking at once: the voices his father had called "demons" because they distorted every word that came into the mind. "No," he said.

"I have," she said, touching his arm. "You are now my eldest son, and we are taking our family home."

"We are home," he said.

"Home," she repeated. "My mother's—"

Something was kicking inside his ribs. Where his heart

should be was a small, clawed animal coming loose. He scrambled up onto his chair and stood towering over his mother. "You can't make me," he shouted. "Because I am going to America with Johan and Yaakov and Aaron."

She stayed on her knees a moment, then tried to get up—too suddenly—and swayed forward as she did. Bernard flushed with shame; she looked like a drunk girl clutching the table edge.

"You are my son, and you will do as I say," she said.

The pressure in his chest built higher. He looked at the woman before him, and for an instant, the curve of her nose, the tiny velvet mole beside her mouth, were as alien to him as the landscapes of Asia in his schoolbook. "I don't know you," he cried, closing his eyes against the sight of her hand rushing toward his face.

"Go to bed," said Gittel. "In the morning we will talk."

At dawn Bernard crept out with his satchel and took the first streetcar to the carpenter's house. Every day he waited for the knock on the door, for the sight of his mother and the three children standing on the step, a cart piled high with belongings. The world seemed to him to have closed its mouth; the gulls, the bright grass, the wide and silent gulf—all seemed to have grown bolder in their colors to judge him.

A week passed. One evening Johan came home from work and took his hand. "Come," he said. "I want to show you something." They took a streetcar out of the city and walked down the street to their own house. It was unlocked. Inside the furniture gleamed, the rug lay bright and soft on the floor, and the pots and pans—always before in the sink—hung clean and polished on the kitchen wall. Under the alabaster lamp was a sheet of paper. *To my beloved Bernard I leave my mother's alabaster lamp, her brass Shabbas candlesticks, and the key ring, so that in America he will remember his mother.* The rest of the letter divided up the household items among the other boys. In an envelope they found the deed to the house.

It was the station porter who had told Johan; he was the last person in the suburb to see Gittel and the three children. He said her fingers quivered when she tried to hand him the four tickets to Berlin. He had never seen her up close before, and told people later that she was a little girl. "Magnificent hands, though," he said. "Like a slender man's, strong and nicely shaped. The kind of hands you don't expect to tremble, and she didn't expect them to either. I could see she was embarrassed, so I said, 'Going for long?' 'Oh no,' she said. 'Just to visit my parents and take the children to a magic show.' She put her hands in her coat pockets. 'I'm terrible about traveling,' she said, smiling."

The silence of the world then was different; it wasn't the silence of waiting, but the kind that comes after a mistake, with disbelief caught in it like a maimed bird. The three oldest brothers swore never to allow their mother's name to cross their lips as long as they lived—not even if she wrote and begged their forgiveness, or became ill. They worked hard, and Johan spoke continually of passage costs and departure dates. And Bernard began to dream. He dreamed he was sitting beside his mother on the piano bench, both of them dressed for his father's funeral service. Suddenly she rose from the bench and gripped his arm. "Come with me," she cried, "into the piano where it's safe." Bernard looked out the window. At the door and all the windows of the house stood a

hundred men in fine suits, knocking politely. He bit his
mother's hand, but she kept her grip, drawing him to her and
into the open piano. The lid came down, suffocating . . .

After school Bernard sometimes went to the station to
listen to the porter, who was still elaborating on Gittel's departure: how she looked, how the three little boys clung about her
asking, "Will there be an acrobat there? Will there be a fat lady
and a thin man? Will they cut somebody in half and make him
come out whole?" Every day the story got longer. The porter
got better tips, and his tongue lightened as if it were a balance
scale tipping in one direction. "Terrible circles under her
eyes," he said. "And the children: I swear the youngest knew
it was for more than three days—"

Such stories the Gittel could tell you—about strangers in
town, or what happened to the neighbors yesterday, or a terri-
fying dream that would haunt you for weeks, as if you yourself
had dreamed it. But when it came to newspapers, she was a
fool. Thank God that's not the case with Rachel, although
from the look on her face sometimes, and the news of the
world, I think: "What's the difference?" She will argue with
me about Gittel, too, but newspapers or not, Gittel wasn't
thinking about current events. She was sleepwalking, imagining the lovely carpets, the curved staircase, her mother coming
down the hall to greet her, her father sitting down to chat with
a student.

I should stop the story here. For one thing, Rachel's bus
gets in any minute, and the way she walks, she'll be here before
I can clear the table of these papers. . . . But I remember how
it used to drive me crazy when Papa began to describe the
tiniest details of Gittel's traveling dress and people and things

he had never seen. He could never get to the end of the story. *Next time,* he'd say, and next time he'd start all over at the beginning, lingering until Mother called us in to supper. Some habits are hard to break, he used to say.

On the train Gittel took her children into an empty compartment, but you know how it is; someone always comes to interrupt your dreams. This time it is an elderly gentleman, the first German she's seen since she got on in Riga. During the first hour of the ride nobody speaks. The children keep their heads lowered, once in a while glancing up at the stranger, who is smart and alternates his gaze between the countryside and his own shoes. You know how the eye roams when you're traveling. Maybe at this moment my own daughter is sitting in the window seat of a bus, a stranger beside her. Any minute he could turn and look at her face and say, "Going home?" The stranger in Gittel's compartment is polite, and Gittel is busy telling her children about magic shows and lace curtains and hot potato kugel. "Grandpa and Grandma have moved," she says, "but I'll take you to look at the old house. She'll have a lunch for us, too. A hot lunch."

She has a nice voice, thinks the stranger. He lets his eye rest on a piece of hand luggage at her feet, and suddenly, coming awake, he sees the name *Shapiro.* He turns pale and leans forward.

"Frau Shapiro?"

She looks at him, startled, and the children hide their faces in her coat.

So much goes through the stranger's mind when he sees the face of the Gittel: a face that cannot shed its innocence, even when the eyes in it look out the compartment window at the new red and black flags in the station windows—seen quickly, because the train goes so fast. The stranger holds out his hand.

"I knew a Shapiro at university," he says. "I am proud to say. I am proud."

He holds her hand too long; he won't let it go even when the conductor comes into the compartment and says: "Passports, please." Her eyes grow dark with surprise.

"Excuse me, please," she says, pulling her hand away, reaching into her bag for her passport.

"Wait," he says.

But Gittel, with a nervous laugh, has handed hers over. She doesn't change expression when the conductor takes a long look at it and says: "You will report to the Bureau of Immigration as soon as you arrive. Your passport needs changes."

The conductor is gone. The stranger wants to tell her something, but her face speaks to him like marble, like a desert statue that knows either everything or nothing.

What can he do but ask her where she is going, keep her in conversation until the train comes into the station? So he asks, and she begins a story. A story about a lovely house, a mahogany mantel, a fireplace, a smoking chimney, a girl who is coming at this moment through the front door, having for once remembered her key; a girl capable, after all, of surprising her mother.

Icarus Descending

Gregory is in the arena five minutes, and in those five minutes every man old enough to have a grown son has stopped by to offer him a friendly word of advice. It's been three months since he left his house, but everywhere the same story. Whether he's on construction, or carnival, or state fair crew, up they come, a little astonished but mostly wise, offering instruction in their specialties: stage-building, tightrope and net repair, light setup. He holds his face perfectly still, refuses to look them in the eye, but up they come, not hesitating at all, as if he's waved them over from a great distance. Now an older man climbs down from the light booth, his legs slow on the rungs. It's August, and the arena air is heavy with fairground dust and humidity, yet the man wears a cardigan, as if to say that where he works, there's another, cooler atmosphere.

"Hello, son," says the man. "Shouldn't you be in school?"

"I'm not as young as I look," says Gregory.

The man smiles, and Gregory knows he has failed.

At dinner he takes a corner window seat, but the man finds him. His name is Matt and he is head light technician for the Wild Bill Carnival of Omaha, which has the concession at the state fair this year. Matt confesses to Gregory that he is not a very good light technician, especially since developing acrophobia. "I lost a boy in Vietnam," he says, making the motion with his hands of a plane going down.

"Wrong profession for an acrophobic," he says, laughing. "I'm glad you showed up. Maybe I can gracefully retire." Matt's hands, which earlier that day had been long and heavy and capable on the dimmer board, tremble. It's the small things that give him away, Gregory thinks. Pickles, olives, peas. Matt lifts his fork and they scatter. Gregory wants to tell him to take a rest, but the older man grips his fork and scoops up the strays so violently that Gregory looks away.

"Now go," Matt says. "And let everybody get acquainted with you."

)

In his duffel bag, Gregory still has the two letters, one from Cal Tech and one from MIT, both of which begin, *We are pleased to tell you.* They were in the mailbox the day he left, and have been in the duffel since he boarded a bus in the Los Angeles Greyhound terminal. He had taken a window seat on the bus so he could watch the landscape empty itself and start over. He watched it turn into straight roads running outward in spokes, evenness running on forever into places nobody could see; into fields that were fans, always opening; and where there were no mountains closing in a valley, no oceans to come to and say, "Well, I guess we're here," as if they had reached the end of the last frontier. He has saved the letters just in case his father finds him. He pictures their meeting to consist solely of his father stopping in the center of the fairground midway, squinting in the dust and glare, and himself wordlessly pulling out the two letters, an actor in slow motion.

Try putting down on paper why you left, someone suggested to him on the bus. An English teacher moving east. It will make you feel better. But he can't. When he thinks of his father, he can barely see him: he is always standing in a darkened room, backlit by the faint light that comes from a hallway lamp. He is slender and pale and looks young for his age, except for the faint purple shadows under his eyes and beneath his fingernails, as if the ink he used for his blueprints has gotten permanently imbedded in his flesh. For years he had come into Gregory's room at night to stand beside the bed, barely breathing while he thought Gregory slept. Gregory, under the covers, kept his eyes closed and imagined what his father was wearing: tweed suit, trench coat, long chestnut-colored shoes with the pattern of tiny holes. He felt his father not breathing and thought, while my father is not breathing, I should not be breathing either.

After a moment, his father would exhale. Then he would whisper an inexplicable phrase. "You are dreaming this, my son," he would say. "There is no one in your room, and never was." He always left suddenly, the cool air, the firm, accountable smell of ink and metal compass going with him.

Gregory lengthened, went long and gangly and tall as his father, though not so pale. He had a rosy skin that seemed always to have a flush beneath it, which a girl named Liz loved. At night he hauled her up through his window and they stared at each other's arms and faces and hair in the faint yellow of the streetlight. They made it a game, touching each other tentatively until they heard the sound of feet coming down the hall. Then Liz ran to the window, Gregory holding her wrists till the last second. She laughed, twisting lightly out of his grip, knowing exactly when to drop to the grass. One night Gregory went so far as to take off his shirt, and lift her blouse over her arms. He was breathless, and could not help tingling with the thought of his father accidentally seeing them. He slowed his motions, letting his fingers get stupid on her bra strap, and when they heard the steps coming down the hall, they could not move apart fast enough. He stood over them, and did not seem to see the girl. She scrambled to the window and out, not wanting to see what a man so calm and cool-skinned might do. Gregory and his father stood face to face, identical in height, and Gregory's father said nothing. He was not wearing a trench coat, but a bathrobe so loose that it might at any moment come undone. He made no effort to cover himself, and seemed to Gregory to be holding his breath as he had all the nights of Gregory's childhood.

"Dad," he said. "Get out of my room. You're dreaming this, because there's no one in my room, and never was."

His father did not answer, only trembled as if he were a fragile vase with a faltering blue light inside. After he left, Gregory waited ten minutes, until he knew he would never catch his breath if he stayed. Outside, the spring air surrounded the house, harsh and soft at once, like a girl twisting out of his grip. He packed his jeans and shirt, and the two letters. Then he gripped the white sill, like Liz, and let himself drop.

❯

After Matt dismisses him from dinner, Gregory does as he is told. He sits on his trailer step so that people can get acquainted with him. He doesn't mind: he's good at being looked at. He's good at holding still and feeling how it is with the people doing the looking. They look at his clothes, his hair, his mouth: waiting to see what he will give away. Meanwhile, he looks slightly to the side and down, to the feet as they pass, to the height of the dust kicked up. A little high means that person is sick to death of newcomers, and wants to tell him so. A little low is timid, with favors to ask. No dust at all isn't what you'd think, isn't obliteration. It's a kind of power: the kind someone gets when he decides he's invisible.

By the time dinner is over and the men have walked by, it's the women's turn. They walk past in twos and threes, each with a different step than she had as she came toward him. Each skirt sways more deliberately from side to side, as if it will swing just so far before heading back the other way. Some walk too carefully, and Gregory closes his eyes to prevent them from tripping on some little twig in front of him.

The last one out is alone: a small, narrow, nervous person with a crop of brown hair she must have cut herself, in a bad mood. She takes long strides that end in abrupt stops, as if she's being yanked in by reins. Gregory takes this as a sign of a certain kind of courage: abrupt, and probably undependable. She is brave now, though. She pushes back her bangs with her small hands, and sits down next to him. She lights a cigarette and offers one to him. He takes it, and lights it from hers, so that she can see he isn't shy.

"So," she says, "what do you think of Nebraska?"

"I'm *from* Nebraska," he says, thinking of the fanning-out roads and fields.

"Is that supposed to be a joke?" she says.

"Not that I know of. Why?"

"Because you're smiling," she says, putting out her cigarette. "I hate it when people smile like they have some secret and you're supposed to guess what it is."

"Don't you have a secret?" Gregory asks her.

She closes her eyes a moment, then stands up to leave.

Gregory is thinking, here's a secret. I am going to close my eyes and pretend that I know you, and that your name is Liz.

)

Gregory has a system for falling asleep. He pictures the workshop in their garage, and his father's back to him, hunched intent over a project at his drafting table. Gregory starts at one end of the garage and works his way across, recalling the name on each cabinet and drawer, each labeled in a precise, backslanted hand. *The handwriting of a genius,* Gregory once said, and his mother smiled, her hand to her mouth. Once Gregory has finished counting, and has remembered each name, he waits for his father's daily question.

"In what situation," asks his father, "is it possible for a person to hang on to the live wire of a cable and not be electrocuted?"

Gregory smiles: it takes him no time at all to answer.

"In the situation of not being grounded," he says. "If you are suspended in the air, with nothing metal on you, and you don't touch anything but the hot wire, you're safe."

"Good answer," says his father, "good and quick." Then he frowns. "Of course, we'll keep this theoretical, won't we, son?"

"Theoretical is your father's favorite word," says Gregory's mother, leaving the garage.

If this doesn't work, Gregory pictures his bedroom, not the way it was when he left, but when he was younger. There are pictures on the wall of a dog, a cat, and a rudimentary building, too primitive to show promise. He closes his eyes and holds still, waiting for the door to open, for the smell of ink on paper, of book dust to enter. He smells the ruler and compass, chill metal in the night air. His father is here, two feet from him and no more, and the silence between them is warm, regular, good. His father stands, and he lies, and in silent agreement they each pretend they are not breathing, knowing that one might overwhelm the other. Gregory, lying in his trailer bed, narrows his face back to what it must have been when he was nine or ten, narrowing it until he hears his father exhale.

"You're a good boy," his father says. "You'd never make your old man look bad, would you?"

)

In the morning it turns out that the brave girl is a trick rider, a bareback artist. She rides an Arabian around the ring, and when the horse rears up, the two of them are one, indistinguishable from one another from up in the light booth or on a catwalk. Sometimes a second horse comes into the ring, and she plants a foot on each, raising her small, muscular arms over her head. She never looks back, never to the side, no matter what position she's in. She sits, or stands, or does a front flip and lands with her feet exactly seven inches apart on the horse's back. All the time she looks in whatever direction is straight ahead for her.

It also turns out that she has a lover, or at least her lover thinks she does. He is a follow-spot operator with dark hair and a laugh too powerful and erratic for the tiny light booth, where he leans in the afternoon over the panels with Matt and Gregory. He is leaning heavily, gazing down into the arena where the girl practices alone, and there is an imbalance to his weight that makes Gregory think he might fall into the ring if the glass walls weren't there to prevent it. He flicks the dimmer switches aimlessly, and Matt's small, compact body twitches slightly. Then the younger man turns from the panel and cocks his head at Gregory.

"You ever worked in an arena this size?" he asks, still looking down into the ring.

"Sure," says Gregory.

"In this line of work," says the man, "there's no such thing as sure. Watch out for yourself."

Then he's gone, out across the upper catwalk to a place Gregory can't see from the booth. The moment he leaves, the little room seems sized right again, and cooler.

Matt is at his best up here. His hands rest on the dimmer switches comfortably: the hands of a professional, loving the surfaces he has made dependable. Squinting across space, he brings up red and brings down blue, crossing fire into ice on the girl below. His feet are planted straight ahead and flat, like the feet of people riding on a jet or a boat, as if straight and flat makes the surface seem more like solid earth. In two days Gregory has not seen Matt on a catwalk. He stays inside the booth, ordering Gregory or someone else out to make repairs. Now a blue burns out high up, near center. Gregory grabs a new bulb and gel.

"I'll go up with you," says Matt. He's behind Gregory, shivering as he puts one foot onto the ladder. "Frank has a little test for newcomers," he says. "Especially the ones that go for Annie."

"Who's Annie?" Gregory asks.

Matt sighs, his face lit to lavender as he gazes down into the ring. "Innocence is bliss," he says.

"I think the phrase is ignorance," corrects Gregory. "I like tests, anyway. You stay here and watch."

"All right," says Matt. "But if anything seems funny at all, jump."

"Jump?"

Matt is grinning now, both feet back inside the booth. "Jump," he says. "You're not acrophobic, too?"

It isn't until Gregory is in the middle of the high catwalk under the burned-out bulb that he sees something shimmering between himself and Annie. If it had been anyone other than Matt who told him, he would not have believed in the net: it is as faint as stars when you stare directly at them. He takes out the old bulb, clamps in a new one, slides the new blue gel across the lightbox. Some cords dangle loose near by, and he pulls a length of duct tape from his belt loop. *Never let a stray cord stay stray,* was his father's line, said with his back furled safely over the drafting table away from Gregory. Here's a problem, a test, his father would say, and Gregory, high above

the ring, is waiting, when he glances up and sees Matt waving
at him from the booth. He starts to wave back and Matt shakes
his head, pointing upward. It's a light tree, unhinged at one
end and swinging toward Gregory, the colored gels all flying
toward him like a row of bright geese. He can lie down flat and
they will miss him, but here is the test. He spreads his arms,
feels the air rush above and below, marveling at the searing
heat that passes through his arms and belly, belly and arms not
knowing there's a net to catch them. Flying, he thinks, this is
what it would be like to not be grounded.

Frank and Annie stand beside the net.

"Now I can say it," Annie is whispering, her voice tight
and small as a drum. "Now I can say that I hate—"

The gels flutter down over Gregory in the net, red and
green and blue. They make a falling curtain, shutting everything out.

)

Annie is waiting for him at five-thirty, when he reaches his
trailer.

"Want to walk?" she asks, pointing toward the north end
of the fairgrounds, where Gregory sees a long line of trees that
could be a park, or a river, he can't tell.

He doesn't pay attention to the direction she takes him.
He concentrates on the swing of her arms, the light, nervous
step that is just enough like Liz's. They leave the midway in
a hot wind, the dust racing up and down the booth corridor,
hurling up cinders and curled leaves and sawdust. They pass
the dart booths and the ping-pong-in-the-fishbowl booths, and
a ride called Bob's Sleds, where a man named Bob sits listening

to an old Buddy Holly tune while counting his ticket rolls for tomorrow's opening. They pass the heavy red and white boxes labeled DANGER/HIGH VOLTAGE, next to the Ferris wheel. It's running now, with nobody on it, and the boxes hum, not knowing. Red and white, they draw the eye: they are alive and asking for attention the way heights and water do. Gregory and Annie cross the parking lot and enter the grove of trees. She sighs and raises her arms the way she does when she is free and triumphant on a horse. Through the trees Gregory sees the reflections of windows, a square of trimmed lawn, and a redwood deck where a man stands, hands on his hips, looking out.

"He's sick," Annie says. "He could have killed you."

"The net was there," says Gregory. "It was just a test."

She looks at him. "It isn't always," she says, and he isn't sure which she means, the net or the test. The late-afternoon light coming through the trees is weak on her arms; it is not a performer's light. Under it her wrists are fragile, light freckles appear, and her elbows are bony under the rolled-up sleeves of a man's flannel shirt. She looks comfortable and glad to be wearing it, even though it probably comes from a man who frightened her. Gregory runs his finger along its edge, along her forearm to her wrist. She draws her breath in sharply and averts her face from his.

"I know what you're thinking," he says. "You're thinking that if you can't see him, he can't see you. Like that game, Olly, Olly Oxen Free."

Her eyelids shut more tightly, barely letting the tears out.

❯

Gregory doesn't want anything, except not to move. Daylight has passed, has been replaced by the faint blue from a backyard lamp. Blue is the color of new love, he thinks, the color that shines in on forbidden places, backyards, bedrooms, shining in on smooth, small limbs before anything happens. It is movement that makes things go wrong, a false move of an arm or leg, a mouth opening when it is perfect, closed. Branches are smart, he thinks. They finger the air over our heads, splitting it infinite and graceful, without striving, as if to say that if you don't touch earth, there can never be an end to you. It is something he would like to tell his father when they meet again. *Dad,* he would say, *I learned something for both of us,* and hold out his hand as if something, an offering, lay upon it. In the grove, Annie has fallen asleep, and he leans over her, watching the shadows finger her cheek, holding his fingers slightly above her face, sure that if he leans more they will touch the glass of a window, or the fiber of a net. He is leaning slow, suspended, when she opens her eyes.

"Oh God," she says. "Somebody's here."

Gregory knows he is supposed to stand up, but he can't shake himself out of his dream. It is like one of his father's tests: how do you let go of perfection, fast and easy? A girl is stumbling, crying, leaving him again, and he is supposed to rise and answer. The man before him is not wearing a trench coat, his hair is not neat and curled back over his collar, nor does the good smell of ink accompany him. He is wearing a bathrobe and slippers, and beneath its skirt Gregory can see a pale slant of flesh, and hair.

"No," he cries. "No!" And he is suddenly taller than the man. He sees a forehead close to his own, a forehead not broad, not intelligent, but narrow and throbbing in one place with a pulse so small it can be hidden and brought out. "Go away," he cries, and the pulse settles, small and tense and contained. He remembers his mother's hand coming up to her mouth. *Theoretical is his favorite word.*

"You're in the wrong backyard," says the man. "I'll give you till the count of three—"

"Dad," cries Gregory. "Can I wake up now?"

The man cocks his head and smiles. "Well," he says. "What do you think?"

It's a question Gregory can't answer right away. He looks all around, at the branches of the trees, at the ground between them, at the fine dust covering the ground, which if he waits long enough will rise and tell him what lies just beyond words. His turning is like a prayer, and when he finishes, he is alone.

)

It is already hot, and Gregory's alarm clock, set for seven, has been shut off. The sheets are gritty with small stones and twigs, and someone is knocking on the trailer door: four times and a pause, four times and a pause. It is a broad-daylight knock, the kind that won't acknowledge it's connected to the night before, the kind that forces you to answer in your best day voice, "Yes, I'm awake."

After a few minutes Gregory looks out the small upper window. A man is walking away, already too far to recognize in the early morning glare. On the floor is a note. "Somebody here to see you," it says. All he can think is that his father would not leave a note like that. His father would sign his name, and explain.

It is the first day, and the parking lot is full. The stock-car races have begun, all of them at once, it seems, their engines blurring into one enormous roar that to someone far away might sound comforting, like water, or wind in the branches of a tree. Already the dust is rising and swirling on the midway, and Bob is at his station, helping families into little ice blue sleds, his *Origins of Rock 'n' Roll* at full blast. The families are obedient, stepping into the little sleds, and for a moment only the dust moves, and the small Swiss flags over the ride station, and Bob moving among the families like a man among manikins. He pulls back the lever and the cars jerk forward, the children's and the parents' heads jerking forward with them, while the rest of their bodies stay still. Hair flutters back, like the flags, as the sleds gain speed around the curves.

People move around this country, Gregory thinks, walking down the midway. People he knew will grow up and settle in towns far away, and bring their children to the fair on a Sunday, on a hot August Sunday just like this. He will recognize them first, but wait for them to turn to him and say, *Hey, aren't you the one who left ———?* It is on a day like this, when the heat is stifling, making everything hold its breath, that, walking down the midway, he will see a tall, slim man in a professorial tweed jacket, stooping to throw a skid-ball. His aim will be precisely taken, and he will barely miss, then turn to make sure that no one has seen.

With five minutes to go till showtime Gregory climbs the ladder to the light booth and joins Matt at the panel. Matt nods, headphones on, his lips pursed in concentration.

"Was somebody looking for me?" Gregory asks.

Matt shrugs. "Houselights down, reds 4, 5, blues 2 and 8,

up. Frank, take Annie on the follow-spot."

Gregory pulls the dimmer switches smoothly as Annie leads the riders into the ring. She's standing up on the Arabian, arms in the air in magenta warmth, the combination of his reds and blues and Frank's powerful spot. She doesn't know or care whose light is on her, Gregory thinks. Her head is high, not looking at anyone, as if at some point, earlier in her life, she had made a deal never to look anywhere but straight ahead.

"I don't believe it," says Matt. "Number four just went out, the whole tree. Frank said they were brand-new bulbs, for God's sake."

"It's okay," says Gregory, already up. "I'll fix them, one at a time, so nobody notices."

"You stay right where you are," Matt answers, wagging his head. "Right after the first show we'll switch off the circuit breaker and let them cool. Then you can go be a hero."

Gregory is digging in the box for replacement bulbs.

"I know what not to touch," he says, and is out of the booth before Matt can say anything else.

❯

Up on the highest catwalk, Gregory marvels at the glare and the heat, at the blues and reds full on his hands; the performers have no idea how hot the lights get. He wonders if his father ever felt something like this in his work, if he ever, when he was young, had the chance to climb this high above a scene. He looks down at the horses and riders spinning around the ring. He can tell Annie because she is first, and because her figure is straighter, more controlled, than the others. She's lying on her back now, looking up, and around and around she goes, bound to the running horse, letting something other than her own motion carry her. That's not something Gregory could do. He wants to wave to her and shout, *Annie catch me, I'm coming down, not bound to anything.* But he knows she doesn't see him, that she is looking at some point between them that he can't see, feeling only the spine of the horse and maybe something else, the spinning of a planet with nothing above or below it. That's her art. The ring is a wide sea and she has learned how to float, how to stay afloat for hours.

Gregory has brought his gloves just in case, but he knows, he knew back in the booth, that this bank of bulbs cannot be too hot. They had all burned out instantly. He peels back the blue gels and the extra bits of duct tape, leaning out slightly from the catwalk.

Matt is on the headphones: "For Pete's sake get off the catwalk," he says. "Use the bracing cable or you'll fry yourself silly."

"Don't worry," says Gregory. "I will if I need to."

The gel is between his teeth now, slightly warm, like the smooth surface of a stone, or a pond on a nice day. He puts in a new bulb but nothing happens.

"Terrific," says Matt. "It's a fuse. Come on back."

"I've got an extra," Gregory answers. "While I'm at it—"

Annie does a front flip and the crowd applauds. She's got her arms flung out again, triumphant, actually smiling at them.

The bracing harness hangs near by. Gregory takes off the headphones and places them on the catwalk. *There can't be anything metal on you*, he thinks. *If you're not grounded, and if you don't touch the neutral wire when you touch the hot, you'll be safe.* He steps into the harness: it swings, goes taut, holds him. Below, Annie is on her back again, going around for the finale. The crowd is on its feet, the faces so small that Gregory can't tell if they're watching her, or if someone who knows where to look has seen the harness and pointed to the boy swinging high over their heads.

Matt looks old from where Gregory is; from above, his face is no longer washed in lavender, but a dark, mottled purple from the mix of blue and red. He is not watching Gregory, but staring down at his light board like a man in church looking down for something he has lost. Gregory wants to hold him in his mind like that, up high in his little glass booth, struggling to be a good technician when something else is swelling in him, forcing itself to the surface.

Gregory is ready now. He hauls himself along toward the cable where the fuse connection is, but he can't seem to get close enough. It's peculiar: what else is the harness for if not to repair the fuse or wire along this line of cable? Then he sees the problem. The cable hooks nearest him are empty; the cables have been moved over two feet, just far enough so a person in the harness could not reach them. For a moment the name *Frank* occurs to Gregory, then vanishes. Big and dark and erratic, Frank is oddly necessary and incidental, like a messenger in a play who is not important in himself, only for what he bears.

Gregory remembers everything his father taught him now: bits of questions on physics, engineering, house-building, and how to answer a question quickly and accurately. How his father kept things neatly labeled and theoretical, kept everything clear between them in daylight so that no one, not even Gregory, could label his hidden, trembling self. In sorrow and love Gregory pulls himself out of the harness, looking down one more time, but the lights are so brilliant that he cannot tell whether the shimmering beneath him is the net, or a reflection of the glittering human activity below. He squints out across the arena, filled with the perfect, certain sensation of knowledge he has only known in dreams: that his father is in the audience, and watching him.

Below, Annie rides on her back, and her lips, though Gregory cannot see them, are opening and closing in warning. A surge of adrenaline washes through him as he realizes that it is at last his turn to perform for her, and for his father. He lifts one foot out of the harness and reaches for the hot wire, feeling, miraculously, only a small tickle of electricity. Dad, he thinks, it's true, and he grips the hot cable with both hands now, the fuse forgotten. It's true, he thinks, and now it is my turn to ask a question. If you were me, what would you do? Go back to the catwalk, or take the descent; slow, free, and full of possibility?

Victrola

She was stubborn from day one. For her, words like fate or
destiny, words we throw around, were as real as the roots of
the live oak, spreading under the sidewalk where no one can
see them but the child who stands directly under the tree,
imagination intact. She didn't know what life intended for
her, but it was obvious to the casual observer that she meant
to have one, since she eluded death and disaster so well, even
when her mother, the beautiful idiot, was managing things. By
the time Francisca was eight years old, she had already survived three Mazatlán epidemics and the stings of two deadly
scorpions. She was also known for her tendency to have fever
dreams that nobody could decipher. It was just after the second scorpion and its accompanying dream that she awoke to
see her father's yellow guitar sailing through the air across
their shed.

The shed, located at the edge of her uncle's *rancho*, was
tiny and dim, its only light coming in thin, brilliant streams

through a crack in the wall, like a badly placed stage light. Even in this light, Francisca's mother was spectacular, with her high, flat cheekbones and one side of her long skirt hiked up to her waist for effect. Her eyes were a smoky olive green, her mouth barely curved and secretive, and when she flung the guitar at Francisca's father, she flexed her wrists with a dancer's delicate arrogance. The father, a former policeman and fine musician, failed his wife as he had failed the police force: unable, at a crucial juncture, to wipe from his face his expression of stunned good nature. He picked up the two halves of his guitar and announced that he was going north to Chicago, where a big plant was opening up. Were they coming with him or not?

Francisca struggled to come awake. Still sick with fever, she had been dreaming that she was a nun, dressed in a magenta habit stained with the pure translucent saffron of the scorpion's curled tail, and that she was flying, fast and low over her uncle's *rancho* and farther, all the way across the border to a town she didn't recognize. She thought she was still dreaming until she saw her father holding the split guitar, its strings dangling. A moment later his hands lifted her from her cot, hesitated, and set her down again.

"For now," he said, "stay here."

❯

When he had been gone four months, Francisca and her mother were passed from the Mazatlán relatives to her mother's sister in Nogales, where Francisca's Auntie Agnes managed an American-owned tortilla factory. The mother and daughter would earn twenty-five cents a day, *American money*,

Auntie emphasized, *so that they wouldn't have to wait a hundred years to find out the son of a bitch wasn't going to send for them.* Auntie never looked directly at Francisca or her mother when she said this, but raised her face to the wall of her office, as if she saw, among the three framed business plaques, something they would never understand. Auntie Agnes was tall, like Francisca's mother, with tapered, polished fingernails and hair that shone like fire embers in the daylight, except for a half-inch at the scalp. Her eyebrows, also red, were plucked so vigilantly that one made perpetual, cynical comment upon the other. Auntie's lips were painted purple, unlike those of Francisca's mother, who had, since the move to Nogales, taken to wearing deep crimson—"for professional purposes," Auntie muttered under her breath.

She didn't stop there. "Your mamma," she said, "has the nerves of a chicken. Without my influence, the two of you would have starved long ago." As she spoke, she gave Francisca's mother a portion of their week's wages, and took from her the dollar they had just received in the mail from Chicago. She tucked the dollar inside a money belt she wore around her waist, giving Francisca's mother a few coins in return. "The day you carry a load of tortillas from one end of this factory to the other without incident," she said, "this is the day you will go north, with my blessing."

)

Francisca waited. All day she traversed the factory's big room, balancing big stacks of fresh tortillas on her head: the higher the better, to make up for her mother's small loads. Passing the little glassed-in manager's booth, she mimicked her mother's dance moves from the Mazatlán American Club, lifting her small hips one at a time. This would show Auntie that *she*, Francisca, could more than make up for her mother's sudden clumsiness, and at the same time allow her to glimpse Auntie's United States behavior. Auntie sat inside the glass booth with her best friend, the American, Señor Jeff. Her feet crossed on her desk, she smoked a thin brown cigarillo and threw her head back to exhale, revealing the ghostly white line of her scalp. Francisca could stand there whole minutes unobserved; it was only when her mother passed the booth, her dainty elbows dangerously raised, that Auntie dropped her feet and hunched forward.

Francisca loved this moment, for no one could look at her mother for long without losing whatever expression was originally intended, and taking on the slack mouth and glazed eye of a Mazatlán American Club patron. This was her mother's particular gift: a neat, compact, narrow body, incapable of stirring jealousy but fully capable of stirring something else: suspense. You looked at her and a terrible, pleasurable fear grew in you—what accident was about to befall her, while she gazed, unconscious of the edge of the stage, at her own slim fingers? Much later, long after she was dead, she would appear this way in Francisca's dreams; a flickering presence on the edge of a theater platform, her face solemn, white, adrift in the dark.

Beautiful and rare, her mother's solemn side came out after nightfall, after supper and prayers in the room they shared, after chores in the big house Auntie had purchased with the assistance of Señor Jeff. At that hour, Francisca and her mother left their room to walk single file to the well.

There, her mother lifted her face to the sky, which instantly responded, opening like a dark curtain pricked with tiny holes for light. The other way to look was toward the long string of lights, low to the earth, that was Nogales, and maybe only a little farther, Chicago. In that direction Francisca could make the world fold over itself until her father appeared strolling on a city street, strumming his yellow guitar with three other gentlemen. They were so close that she could hear the loose gravel crunching beneath their heels, and hear one say to the others, "It is time for a love ballad, a lament." They all laughed good-naturedly. This was her father's cue.

"Wash, Francisca," said her mother, and she did. They walked back, single file, as if following an invisible line, back into their room with its two cots side by side: the chamber pot under her mother's side, the washing basin and pitcher they were supposed to use under Francisca's.

It was at this hour that Francisca loved her mother most, loved her the way one conspirator loves another, desperately, as out of the pocket of her skirt her mother brought the cotton pouch, spilling its contents onto her cot. The next night it would be Francisca's turn to spill the coins, all things being fair and equal between conspirators. The difficulty that arose nightly was whether you counted your money before saying your prayers, in which case you prayed with dirty hands, or prayed, then counted your money, in which case you would be unclean and have to pray again. Francisca imagined that Auntie Agnes prayed and counted simultaneously, in order to be what she called *efficient,* but she did not mention this to her mother. Her mother disliked the sound of the American word *efficient.*

At last came the night Francisca's mother spilled the coins onto her cot and smiled. "We've done it," she cried. "We don't need either of them—we can get to Los Angeles on our own."

"Los Angeles," cried Francisca. "I thought it was Chicago."

"Oh, they aren't that far apart," said her mother. "Anyway, what's your hurry?"

In the morning it appeared that Auntie had read her mother's mind. After breakfast she rose from the table and pressed both hands down upon it just as Señor Jeff sometimes did in the glassed-in booth. "I have gone to the trouble of purchasing your train tickets and signing the necessary papers," she said. "And you have, by now, earned the little something you will need when we arrive in Santa Ana."

"We?" cried Francisca's mother. "And where is Santa Ana?"

Auntie smiled. "If it were not for my influence, your child would now be dancing like a you-know-what in Mazatlán. Look for me when you get off the train, Francisca. I'm putting you in charge. Wave to me the minute you see me and Señor Jeff, who has been kind enough to give me the management of his tortilla factory in Santa Ana."

"How are you getting there, Auntie?" whispered Francisca, unable to imagine the tall figure of her aunt taking any human means of transportation, but simply appearing, without anybody's assistance, before a stand of fluttering palms.

"Señor Jeff is taking me in his automobile," said Auntie, not looking at either of them. "Unfortunately, it is quite cramped for more than two."

)

That night, the mother and daughter stood at the well a long time. Francisca's mother pressed her hands to the well's curved stone lip, arching her back as if she intended to pass through the dark curtain and up into the points of light behind it.

"What are we waiting for?" she cried. "Who is watching?" She held out the cotton pouch, heavy as a ripe fruit. "For me, it will be a new dress. Black, I think. Black silk." In the dark, her mouth hinted a mystery. "And what will you buy, Francisca?"

Francisca looked toward the low-lying lights of Nogales. *Give us something, Capitán José,* the men would just now be saying to her father, standing beneath the festive colored lights, gravel crunching beneath their heels. *Give us something sad, to capture the hearts of ladies.*

"A new guitar," she said. "To give Papa when we get to Chicago."

"I have a better idea," said her mother, frowning. "Wait and see."

)

The train to Los Angeles was dark green with gold letters, green and gold just like Auntie Agnes's best traveling suit. Auntie stood beside a long black car at the station, waving frantically at them to open their compartment window.

"It looks just like a hearse," whispered Francisca's mother. "And on top of that, she has the mouth of a fish—she shouldn't wear that color lipstick." She leaned forward, giggling like a young girl. "Here, sweetheart, have a wonderful one, have a little volcano." She held out a *jalapeño* from their lunch basket. "Look for me when you get off the train, Francisca, you're in charge. I will be waiting for you with handcuffs, so don't move too fast!"

Francisca wanted to giggle with her mother, but her own pleasure was too solemn, too exquisite: it burned in her throat like the *jalapeño* she did not take. On her lap she held the Victrola they had purchased in town that morning, and a record of her mother's favorite opera, *Carmen.* Once in a while a chill ran up her neck—what if her father did not like the gift? He always said, *I like the sound of music up close, from in here,* and pointed to the dark well of his guitar. "You misunderstood him," her mother had explained that morning at the shop. "Nobody loves *Carmen* like your father. Nobody."

Since its purchase, Francisca had not yet wound the machine: for now it was enough to hold it on her lap, to feel the solid, heavy weight of the wooden box, the silver arm, and the horn, not quite as big as she had always imagined, but its silver mouth wide enough, after all, to allow her mother to put her face into it and cry deliriously down the tube, "Hello in there, my serious child, are you still with us?"

Her mother did not wave to Auntie until the train began to move, and then, as it gathered speed, she leaned forward and with a squeal of pleasure opened the windows. .

"Now," she breathed. "Now we can have some music!"

)

Later, she could remember exactly how many times she had to crank the Victrola's handle, the exact ache of her right arm above the elbow until she heard the first scratchy notes of the overture wavering in the air, and her mother, setting down the basket of food, rose in the swaying compartment they had all to themselves, lifting her slim hands high.

"Oh, Carmencita," murmured her mother, shuffling her feet in small flat steps unlike those in the Mazatlán American Club dances. She moved her fingers too, subtly, turning the palms inward, gazing at them as if they were mirrors. She was so absorbed in her dance that it was Francisca, designated keeper of the Victrola, who, looking out at the desert beyond the train windows, saw him first. She saw him not as a whole, solid person in the doorway where he stood watching, but as a ghost man, imprinted somewhere between the glass of the window and the scrub-dotted endlessness of the desert.

"Mamma," Francisca said calmly. "There is a man outside."

She expected her mother to stop and collapse neatly and quickly as a pair of scissors. Her mother did not. She turned to the compartment door, her hands still upraised and holding the invisible castanets, revealing the perfect contours of the black silk.

"Bravo, bravo," cried the man. "*Carmen* on the train to Los Angeles!" He opened the compartment door and stepped inside, taking off his hat with a gesture so grand he threatened the Victrola's horn. Francisca jerked toward the window, sending the overture into an uneven, drunken cascade. She froze, the music righted itself like a ship, and after what seemed an endless moment, her mother at last lowered her arms. All of this took too long, giving the stranger time to swing his straw suitcase into the overhead rack.

"J. S. Gold," he shouted over the music, holding out his hand to Francisca's mother.

She declined the hand but followed with an odd little curtsy Francisca had never seen before. Her mother turned to her and motioned imperiously toward the Victrola. Pain crowding her chest, Francisca lifted the silver arm, watching the black disk run slower and slower.

The stranger was covered with a fine layer of reddish dust: his pale suit, his mustache, and his wavy reddish hair seemed carved out of a single stone, like the statues in the church courtyard. He was tall and broad-shouldered, with a forehead that went up and up, and cavernous brown eyes that roved over the compartment and the desert outside as if in search of possible entrances, possible exits. In the midst of his search, he stopped and looked at Francisca and her Victrola, and into his eyes came a round, childlike astonishment that made Francisca glance away.

"Forgive me, I've crashed your party," he said, bowing to her. "How about, in return, a little magic? It's a cheap night-club trick, I admit, but I have aspirations. Watch closely."

From his dusty pocket he pulled a Coca-Cola bottle and a quarter, his gestures intimate and precise, like her mother's at night in Nogales, pulling out the pouch of coins. Her mother's eyes were narrowed now, watching the coin.

"Feel it," the man said to Francisca. "Go ahead and bite it if you want."

Francisca shook her head. Her mother took the coin between her fingers and looked at the man, shrugging as he took it back. He showed them how it would not fit into the bottle, then said again, "Watch." The coin dropped into the bottle with a soft thud.

Francisca's mother sighed. "You are well-to-do."

"My parents are," he said hurriedly. "But I'm starting out on my own, with no more than a quarter, so to speak." He looked for a moment at Francisca and her mother and the desert. "I would trade lives with you in a minute," he said.

His words rushed over Francisca like a hot wind that picks up everything in its way and steals it. She looked out the window toward the passing desert. *Make him go away now,* she chanted to herself, moving her lips to make the spell work.

"See what I mean?" said the man, patting the seat beside him so that Francisca's mother at last sat down. "Look at your little girl there, how quiet, how confident she is. She talks to the desert—it doesn't worry her, all that terrible space. Let me tell you something. My parents can't stand the desert. They don't know anything about it and neither do I. But you! You can dance in front of it. I'd like to do that—"

Francisca looked across the compartment in time to see her mother looking straight into the stranger's eyes. He stopped talking, and for the moment you had to like him: his expression was like her father's when he moved his fingers across the frets of his guitar, reverent and a little afraid, not quite sure if the instrument was under his power, or he was under its. *Maybe you're not bad,* she said to herself, moving her lips in order to undo the spell. She could not look at her mother: it was like looking up into the nighttime sky at Auntie's house, the curtain torn in places, but mostly dark.

"Your little girl doesn't trust me," said J. S. Gold, looking again at Francisca. "She thinks I am going to steal you away from her. Tell her that nothing can steal you."

Francisca shook her head; a warm ache welled up behind her eyelids. *That's not it,* she wanted to whisper to him, without her mother hearing. *Do you know how far Chicago is? That's where we're supposed to be.* She gripped the sides of the Victrola and leaned mutely toward him. But he was looking at her mother: she was apparently trying to say something, and her hesitation, the way she suddenly looked down at the swaying floor, must have moved him.

"I don't see why not," he cried. "Why shouldn't we live the way we please? I mean, why should Mother mind if the two of you come back with me?"

"Señor Gold," said Francisca's mother, still looking at the swaying floor. "Would your parents be in need of a housekeeper?"

)

Until that moment, Francisca had not thought about her mother's choice of a black silk dress; in the shops her mother had complained that the most beautiful dresses were always in black, probably to give young widows some consolation. Her smoke-colored eyes were brilliant as she changed out of her old skirt and blouse and cut free the price tag from the silk suit she would wear, on her days off, for the next forty years, her back perfectly straight and her eyes fierce with frustration that the costume donned for escape should cling to her forever. Already her pride was taking shape—in the shop, and then in the hurtling train, as she sat beautifully upright in the compartment while other passengers stood in the corridor, shading their eyes to look out at the blazing, tinted horizon, each wanting to be first to catch a glimpse of change: of the cool bit of blue that would be the Pacific, or any landmark at all, even a cactus standing spindly and dark against the light.

In the compartment, too, something interfered with the desert light—something as new and as weightless as black silk broke the perfect, uncomplicated edge of the horizon. Francisca's mother had risen and buried her face in her hands.

"I wasn't going to tell you, Señor Gold," she said, nudging Francisca's foot with her own. "But I am a widow, three months now."

Señor Gold rose too, his hat held close to his chest, and began talking to Francisca's mother in low, serious tones. Now Francisca saw it: the solemn, hidden, nightfall expression on her mother's face—the familiar blank look she had when she threw the guitar, or hovered at the edge of a stage, and in Francisca arose an answer: that her mother had no right to wear black, no right to change their direction.

Under her fingers the Victrola was cool, solid, more real than her mother or the man now leaning urgently toward her, writing something on a scrap of paper. She remembered something her mother had once said: if you wanted to get your father's attention, play music. Play it so loud he can't hear himself think, and eventually he will forget what he was doing and pay attention to you. That's how he came to pay attention to me.

Francisca wound the Victrola fifteen times and let the heavy silver arm down, with deliberation, on the record. She readied herself; now the two of them would stop behaving like children, would freeze in their places like statues.

But as the music began, the stranger rose and bowed deeply to her mother.

Even then, as young as she was, Francisca knew there was something beautiful and right in their dance, but not for years would she understand her own part in it: how her hand on the Victrola's silver arm, hoping to stop them, took them farther along a path that would turn out to be as wide and full of hidden consolations as the desert. Señor Gold's hand pressed against the small of her mother's back, guiding her expertly in the compartment. His hand, up close, was square and lightly freckled, the nails clean and trimmed, and when Francisca's mother gripped his wrist and swept it lightly across her thigh, he brought it back up swiftly, to the exact, safe center of her back.

Francisca watched. She felt how heavily the Victrola weighed between herself and this man, as if with it she were drowning out everything he might have said to her, and she to him. She must have moved a little, setting the music wavering, for suddenly he turned her mother around and faced Francisca himself, with a look so intent and familiar that he barely had to lift his hand from her mother's back.

"Join us," he whispered.

And she did.

Still Life

Contrary to everything my mother has told me, I believe Tante Rose was born in the Midwest on a brilliant afternoon, when the sunlight probed every leaf on the big elm in their parents' front yard. She died on a day like that, in California, where sometimes the sunlight over the desert reaches the darkest parts of the ocean, and you can imagine that if you dared look, everything, all the way to the bottom, would be revealed at once. It's easy to forget about that clarity, for in a kind of homage to Tante Rose, Mother closed the blinds in our guest bedroom, making it so utterly dark that when the ambulance men came to take Tante, I had to squint to see her tiny, childlike form float away from me and up into that violent exposure.

It is with this same obstinacy about the dark that, when Mother tries to tell her sister's story, she winds up with only a fragment or two. Beginning or ending, she seems to bend over her words like a gypsy over cards she herself can barely see. Of course I am not being fair; she was twelve years younger than Rose, and raised by parents whose faces, in photographs, bear their own lost childhoods like the shock from a stove burn. And so the pictures containing my mother are like small, safe nets in which she is caught: a rosy, blond, pampered child whose underwear and socks have been allowed, for the day, to lose their elastic. Later, of course, she would conquer all that, but this is who she was when her older sister escaped the lovely, neat house in West Lafayette. Escaped, says Mother, though not before tightly lacing the old-fashioned black boots Grandmother made her wear, when all the other girls had long since begun to wear the slim, handsome pumps of the thirties. Mother remembers this: Rose, on a dark winter morning, tucking a nickel into the finger of one black glove, then bending to whisper in her ear: "This is how working girls keep their carfare safe in the big city."

And she was gone.

Maybe this is why, in my mother's telling, it is always a dark winter morning in a Northern city when Rose gets up and walks to the El, wearing black gloves and a black wool coat, her hair bobbed short in the fashion of the day—though heavy braids had suited her face better, so serious and frowning like one of her mother's generation, eternally clutching a ticket for a further passage. Rose has been lucky enough to find a job in the city, lucky to be able to write a letter home that says how beautifully everything has turned out, how sorry if I frightened you, money forthcoming. She feels her luck at those moments we are told are inconsequential, as when she grips the tram pole with both black-gloved hands, or searches her own eyes in the window as the car goes into a tunnel. On those rides she takes herself in greedily, composing and recomposing the already-sent letter in her mind, while behind it, a secret thought stands with its hands neatly folded, a passenger within the passenger: *Now I am free to live, and to suffer greatly, romantically, as my mother did not.*

But not yet. For the time being she is content to rise each morning and take down her freedom in a series of little notes: the sputter of the radiator, the three-minute egg knocking against the inside of the saucepan in the perfectly square kitchenette. She steps out in the old-fashioned boots she is not quite ready to relinquish, to ride the El into the city where she is a medical stenographer. All day there are more little notes, little barriers she knows she could knock over in an instant if she so chose: headphones, perfect posture, the small lap-typewriter. Her mother would approve if she could see her here, and so Rose has the delicious self-consciousness of the runaway made good, still hiding, breathing in short gasps, locating the smallest, most obscure corners in terminals, rooming houses, cafés.

Of these, her favorite is Sam's Lunch Counter, where Sam has come to reserve for her the back table, and a chair that does not wobble. She is *Tea with Lemon, White Toast* at ten o'clock, and the daily special at noon, no matter what. For days on end she brings with her the same enormous book—Sam can never see the title, only that it is a heavy book with a rough surface—a book that will not end easily or soon, and that will complicate and complicate until the ending does not matter. What thrills Rose is not so much what's in the book as the bare physical fact of its lying before her in a strange place, a book from her mother's house. Inscribed by someone to someone else, it has managed to reappear in this city that is, for her, a dream wedged between two darknesses. She has tea in the thick white mug Sam brings to her table; she admires the outfits of the other working girls; she eats her sandwich and turns each page of the book with an almost unbearable presence of mind, as if she is not only experiencing it, but is also an old woman looking back on her life, holding it beautifully immobile in her hands.

In such a state she falls in love for the first time. I am expecting it to be Sam, for which Mother eyes me quizzically. Of course not, she says; he is a boy her own age, who works in another department and sees her through the glass between their offices. Rose looks up through the glass, too, and sees the young narrow face, the firm energy of his hands as he lifts parcels, makes notes on a chart. And faintly, too, in the glass, she sees her own reflection as she did in the windows of the El, the dark unsmiling eyes that beg for a fate of cinematic proportions, when everything in her experience has been fixed to run the other way.

My picture of them before their marriage and the war is not of the two linking arms to walk in the snow, but of Rose alone at Sam's Lunch Counter, still reading the same big book and glancing up at the windows, where at any moment he might pass by and see her. She is always alone in my picture of her, always waiting for him to turn the corner and meet her in the terrible suddenness of that kind of love, a pointed flame of anticipation.

Starting to see Rose, I no longer hear my mother's voice telling the story but see Mother, too, as she must have been then, eleven years old, lying on her bed in the white upstairs room of her parents' house, a dappled figure on the coverlet in the afternoon sun, wishing herself into her sister's life. Mother is slimmer, and she, too, has a pair of practical black shoes in her closet. When she lies on that bed, the sound of Grandmother's voice is far enough beneath her that she can imagine herself in the city with Rose and her fiancé, riding the streetcar to the World's Fair, her own nickel tucked cool and silvery into the finger of one glove. She is a little dizzy, so both of them hold her hands and point things out to her, and at one moment, the young man, without any warning at all, puts his hands about her waist and lifts her high into the air above the crowd. For a moment she floats effortlessly above the myriad heads—the chestnut, raven, auburn, all shining, each hair defined as a perfect living strand—and she closes her eyes against any change. Fighting something like gravity, she slows her own descent, finding herself at last on a white bed like her own but wider, more brilliantly white, where the three of them rest, not separate at all, but sister, brother, sister.

Mother is the flower girl at their wedding, and it having been only seven weeks since the courtship began, they are breathless still. Mother is too, seeing not their faces but the way their hands and lips can barely meet during the ceremony, as if the slightest brush of flesh is painful. The next day the young man enlists and is gone to the Pacific. In a month, the family will learn that he is in an infirmary with a minor infection Rose will not name. He will be home soon.

She must have met him at the train station, but neither Mother nor I can imagine it, nor can we imagine him telling her he has been cured, that it won't touch her. We see her alone, awakening before him in the early morning dark, stepping out of bed and out of the house before he stirs, going to Sam's for breakfast now as well as lunch. Now she bends closer to the book she has brought, and the dark print on the white page, the steam rising from her cup, all force themselves upon her to keep her from glancing up. They have made an arrangement that he should not be home in the evening when she arrives from work; he is out at a club with friends home on leave. Then one night she comes home to find him sitting at the kitchen table. One shoulder is slumped and there is a quizzical expression on his face, as if he was expecting a blow. He is twenty-five years old and death leaves no mark, no bruise on his narrow face, only an expression of betrayal she cannot, will not, fathom.

In the boxes of books, papers, and photographs pushed to one side of our guest bedroom, the biggest bundle seems placed there as a false clue, something to throw us off the track. There are too many photographs, all documenting the series of pleasure trips she took after the war. They are elaborately framed, hand-tinted, and Rose's cheeks are in a constant, delicate blush. She is always in a group of men and women, all talking at once, when the shutter clicks. In photograph after photograph, something is wrong; she is too close to center frame for my Tante Rose—too close until I notice the slight outward lean of her body, the only sign that her friends have dragged her into the light against her will. Caught like that, Tante Rose is at a loss. Her bewilderment sets itself in a new slant of the eyes, a small, stiff, foxy smile that fools the photographer asking her to chat with a girlfriend on the Canadian train, to hold up binoculars and gasp at the great snowy shoulders above Lake Louise. It is not until a new person appears in the photographs that Rose remembers herself, that she lifts her face to the camera and lets her eyes open wide and dark with a child's grievous desire for experience.

He is a big man in a fur coat in one of the Lake Louise pictures, a full-length fur coat and a fedora, with dark eyes set in a sweet, sad, heavy face. On the back of the picture the name *Pincus* is written in light brown ink, and it is easy to see him being introduced to her at a travel-club meeting, swamping her small, dry hand in his, breathing his name to her in puffs of frosty air. *Pincus Rosen,* chants their host, *one of our most celebrated art historians.* Pish, tosh, says Pincus, and Rose lets her hand rest easily in the enormous warmth of his, not considering whether she will ever see him again, let alone marry him.

He appears in more photographs, but never the summer ones. He is always in a fur coat or an overcoat, the fedora slanting down over his bearlike face, his brown eyes gleaming. There is an abundance to him that she might have at first mistaken for wealth, that of an entrepreneur who, taking off one pigskin glove, would sport a diamond ring on his little finger. Gradually there appear photographs of the two of them alone and one, finally, of the two of them on a ship's deck, the whole picture tilting with a larger motion we cannot see. Rose is leaning again, but this time toward Pincus, with a desire so slow and unknown even to her that it is imperceptible as anything more than the magnetism of a larger body for a smaller one. Pincus is inescapable. He is father, brother, lover; a great, heavy man whose wintry breath is kind, and whose own ending sleeps on hidden cushions in his heart.

After their elopement, Pincus's arm is always around

Rose's shoulder. She is fragile, getting smaller, losing herself in his generosity as if it is a lullaby. At night they look together at art books larger than the books Rose once carried to Sam's Lunch Counter: self-portraits of Rembrandt in whose glance you can read what you like, great success, great disappointment; in whose dark backgrounds there lies a mystery richer to Rose than the sensual textures of velvet, the points of light on lace, that Pincus lingers over. Pincus draws Rose closer, turning the page to a Venus all scallop-curved from breast to thigh, but she has somehow gone past him. She glances away, then leans toward the book with the impulsiveness of the very young or the very old. This one is better, she whispers, turning the page to Michelangelo's *Creation of Adam,* in which, between the hand of God and the hand of Man, there is a hairline fracture in the solid surface of the Chapel ceiling. She looks up at Pincus, laughing, and he bows his head, acknowledging defeat more fully than she can guess, not knowing that he is twenty years her senior and that something is quietly spreading in his body, a tiny crack nobody can see.

It was during this time that Mother met Pincus, at a moment when her life was in danger of holding its adolescent shape forever. She was fifteen, her hair bright and short on a delicate neck, her eyes green and on their way to foxy like Rose's, with the question perennially in them, and perennially denied. She was just defiant enough to have thrown the practical black shoes in the ashcan behind their house and purchased, trembling, a pair of apricot pumps, their slender straps curving around her ankles. Her fingers slipped every time she tried to buckle a strap, and looking down, ready to step out the door, she could hardly believe those were her own feet. That was when the letter arrived inviting her to visit in the city and when, after a fierce argument with her mother, she packed her lightest summer dresses, and was gone.

Why Rose put them together, alone, at the museum, Mother does not say, and purses her lips so that I cannot inquire further. It doesn't matter: now I know who she was, fifteen in her pale pumps and dress, gloves and a low hat, walking through the museum with the great Pincus, whose very overcoat breathes a kind of sleepy power over her, making her sense the faint heat of her skin in the palms of her hands, under the perfect gloves. They move slowly through the rooms, Pincus's face moistening so that he must dab at it gently, though he will not take off the coat. There is something, however, she must see before they go, and they walk through rooms of portraits until they arrive before a painting and he stops, wipes his forehead and says, *now, there.*

How long does it take for Mother to recognize her future self, to accept the nude's long, languorous thigh and curve of hip, the absolute nakedness of a throat when a single golden collar of jewels lies upon it? The man beside her is motionless, yet a knowledge that is not quite a threat moves between them and the picture like a current of air. How long does it take, and how does Pincus know when to step away from the girl and the painting to appraise her with a look that she knows, in the instant before she blots it out, is not lascivious at all but a cool shaft of wisdom that has somehow, by accident or not, traveled to her through a pair of heavy, sensual lips?

"Don't let them stop you from becoming *this,*" he says, and walks away.

She does not immediately turn ash white and go down, in

a heap of pale apricot, on the museum floor, nor does she decide, immediately, never to speak to him again. There is a moment of recognition before the rest, when something gets through to her, before convention, their relations, her sister, her mother, flood her, and she responds in the only way she has been trained: by fainting in a public place.

The next morning Mother will not speak to Rose or Pincus, even when Pincus himself questions her. Her face is stark white, her eyes a snapping green that will not face his for more than a second. She wears a sweater over her dress despite the summer heat. Fiercely, uselessly, she thinks of Grandmother, who will be downstairs dusting the staircase and the sideboard when she arrives. Mother will surprise her, rushing toward her, begging to be enclosed in her house, her arms.

Between Rose and Pincus the incident is never discussed, perhaps because there was some secret, deep collusion between them in the awakening of my mother. In any case it is soon forgotten, for within a month something new has at last gained entrance and is sitting between them on the sofa, waiting to see what they will do with the knowledge of death.

They do what they have always done in the evenings. They look at the great books, at the masters, and now, too, one other thing. Pincus is teaching Rose how to work with pastels. Not oils, not watercolor, but pastels: chalky, delicate, *her* medium, he says, smiling. Rose outlines a pear, a nectarine, a bunch of purple grapes; and for Pincus, lover of light, she allows a silver-gray point to appear on the upper edge of each globe. She rubs a little with the side of her palm, and the salmon, the magenta, and the lavender remain on her wrists for days. She copies still lifes from the big book, and one day, when she is ready, she sketches Pincus. We do not know what season it is, but in it he is wearing his great winter coat and the fedora, and his eyes peer out at us with the ambiguous wisdom of a Rembrandt who cannot decide whether he is ready for death, or whether there is, in fact, something still left to say. If he is looking at Rose, he is trying to tell her something she will need to know after he is gone: that if it is too late to grow up, it is not too late to hold still and let others gather around you, remember you, learn from you.

After Pincus there are no more photographs. There are visits to an apartment in a Southern California town next to ours—an apartment in which there is a kitchenette, a small bedroom, and a stack of art books on the glass coffee table, where I will sit for hours tracing my finger over the hairline crack between the hand of God and the hand of Man. And there will be a day, once a year, when my mother passes me into the hands of Tante Rose. It feels like a conspiracy between the two of them: that day when Mother with great ceremony packs my overnight satchel and bends down to me, her creamy skin smelling of *home, home,* and whispers, "Later, you will be glad I sent you."

The Bonbon Man

For a long time we lived in a town famous for its mysterious Spanish mansions and high hedges, for its twisted streets with the lovely names of Rosalind and Saint Alban. It seemed to me a deliberate act against the imagination that we lived in the newer part of town, where the houses were ranch style, the lawns crabgrass or dicondra at best, and the streets wide and given obvious names: California, Virginia, and so on. I knew everyone on our block, and almost everyone on the blocks behind and before. Those I didn't know, like the Candyman, I stayed well away from, to prevent their being dragged down to the knowable by a careless adult remark such as, "Oh, you mean that nice widower, Mr. So-and-So." The possibility of my father or mother conferring upon the unknown the name Simmons or White depressed me no end. I was beginning to think that the whole point of adulthood was to seek out the inexplicable and expose it.

George Miles was thirteen and well on his way to adulthood. He was accomplishing it not so much by exposing mysteries, as by criticizing mine and coming up with alternatives that were way over my head. He also asked me probing questions about my future at a time when no one else seemed to notice that I had one. It was nerve-wracking. He had a bony face and deep-set black eyes that stared during the contests and at other times, too. Whenever he said anything to me, whether it concerned the creamed corn on my lunch plate or a ghost we had invented in the abandoned lot, he gazed into my eyes with frightening intensity, as if he would bore into my heart and worm out secrets I didn't know I had.

Summers we played together: statues, where one person shouted "freeze" and the other posed in a strange and marvelous stance. I loved the game not only for the poses, but because when I stopped moving, I experienced the pleasant sensation of being visible and invisible at the same time. In parks, people walked around statues without really seeing them, and you could imagine that inside the plaster was a person, aware of everything going on around him, but unnoticed by others.

By late August George had suggested that this was a juvenile activity. He preferred to explore the mazelike streets of the old part of town, "broadening our horizons," he said, by stopping at a mansion and inventing a history for its inhabitants. I turned out to be bad at this. Everything I invented had to do with my family or me. George was irritated all out of proportion and continually pressed me to be more original, to strike out on a new path. Everything he said lately left a little pool of silence behind it; he was becoming a genius and was about to leave me behind. When I mentioned this to my mother she sighed and laid her hand on my head.

"Sweetheart, your friend Georgie comes from a troubled home," she said.

"Do you have to come from a troubled home to be a genius?" I asked.

She looked at me. "We don't want you to be a genius," she said. "We just want you to be happy."

One day George brought me before a thick hedge on Saint Alban, and pointed out a long drive, at whose end was a house partially obscured by trees, with a miniature observatory on its roof.

"I'll start," he said. "In the observatory is an old scientist. Every night he escapes through the top of the telescope into the sky, and becomes young again. All night he travels across the universe having adventures, and nobody, not even his wife, knows where he goes."

I was unable to think of anything. "She sits up all night," I said at last, "worrying whether he took his slippers. He is not a conscientious person."

"No," said George. "You're supposed to go with the scientist into space."

I was afraid to look at him: he would be staring. I thought how pleasant my own room was at this time of day, with the brilliant summer light filtering down through the leaves of the Clarks' live oak, dappling the bed where I lay, a beautiful sad girl locked in a room with only a music box for company. "I have to go now," I said abruptly.

"We'll try again tomorrow," said George.

❩

That night in bed I let my thoughts turn to the Candyman. He was my special province, as no one else was interested in him. No one had ever seen him, not even my parents, as far as I could tell. The only time he came up in conversation was at Halloween, when someone at school inevitably brought up his horrible crime. He lived on the street behind ours, in a pink house on the corner, and was supposed to be paralyzed from the waist down, unable to leave his electric wheelchair. It was said that years ago he made his own caramel apples and popcorn balls, and once lured a little girl my age and size into his house. She was not seen again. I asked my father if this was true and he shrugged. He said it was never a good idea to accept homemade candies at Halloween: razor blades and poison might be inside them, and he forbade me to ring the Candyman's doorbell. My mother nodded her agreement, and I watched her closely, for there was sometimes a hesitation in her responses to questions about the Candyman that made me think she knew something more. "God knows what's true and what isn't," she said dreamily on one occasion, and it occurred to me that the Candyman might be a former Nazi. All of her dreamy moods had to do with our being Jewish. On Friday nights she spoke in aphorisms, sighed dramatically, and reveled in candlelight, turning off the dining room lights so that my father complained he couldn't see his dinner. I relished these moods as if they brought an exotic scent or taste into our house.

In any case, I didn't really want to ring the Candyman's doorbell. It was enough to walk on the opposite side of the street, glancing at the closed, pale blue draperies of the picture windows; at the short crabgrass lawn that hadn't been watered in years; at the flagstone path sunk at various angles into the grass. Inside the house it would be dark and damp as a forest, as a wooden shack where old men waited for you to walk by. Forward the small electric wheels would roll, their spokes clicking until the door swung open (remote controlled) and the victim in her yellow satin tutu and cat-mask was pulled into the house by an irresistible wind. What happened next I couldn't say: I felt my heart beat all out of rhythm and I couldn't get it to smooth out. I lay on my back so that nothing, absolutely nothing would surprise me.

Of course, George would disapprove. "The Candyman is old hat," he would say. "The real challenge, the really difficult thing, would be to go with the scientist into outer space."

I closed my eyes for the attempt, but what came to my mind was the scientist's wife, eighty years old, with pure white hair and a papery pink skin so fragile it looked ready to be shed. She was not inside the observatory, but in a courtyard behind the tall hedges, hanging underwear upon a clothesline. A huge basketful of underwear sat on the grass, and she went along the line, clothespins in her mouth and in her apron pockets, snapping each pair of shorts to the rope before moving on.

In the morning my heart was still beating fast and I felt guilty, as though I had spoken out loud without meaning to. It had something to do with George, for when I met him at the corner of California Street, I couldn't look at him directly.

"Ready?" he asked, beginning to walk in the direction of Saint Alban and the observatory.

"No," I said. "I have to sell Girl Scout Cookies."

He gazed at me, chewing a little on his lower lip, a signal that had always frightened me. This time, however, it made him look sick and old and faintly disgusting. As I walked away, my chest ached dully, as if with an old and worn out sorrow that someone else had used.

This feeling accompanied me up the long incline of the street behind ours. When I reached the corner I crossed over and stood exactly in the center of the first flagstone of the pink house.

"He has white hair," I whispered, my voice strangely immodest in the neighborhood silence. "Like the scientist's wife, his skin is pink and soft, the color of peppermint taffy. He sits right there, behind the front window drapes, a blanket across his knees even in August. He has air-conditioning, and he loves his blanket, because it makes him feel like a harmless old man. A little white dog sits on his lap, and he talks to the dog in French. *'Parlez-vous Française, Pooch?'* he says, and sometimes his wife walks past them into the kitchen, but the Candyman keeps talking to the dog. Mrs. Candyman considers learning French; she has even bought a book, but every time she starts it she gets sleepy, and has to make a pot of tea and cookies. She offers these to the Candyman and goes back to the kitchen, and the Candyman sits all day before the window, watching us come home from school. He is choosing his victim."

When I stopped, the silence and heat of the afternoon seemed to expand and surround me. What if it were Halloween, and the little girl had gotten separated from her brother? She was wearing her yellow satin tutu with the black cat-mask and she had never heard of the Candyman. He came to the front door in his wheelchair and held forth a tray of gleaming caramel apples.

"As she reached forward to take one," I said aloud, "he wheeled his chair further and further back down the dark hallway, and she, hypnotized by the apples, followed him—"

"The Seduction Scene," said a voice close to my ear. "Never have I heard anything more trite."

For a moment he was unrecognizable, his face a blur but for the two black eyes, burning feverishly.

"So," said George. "This is how you sell Girl Scout Cookies."

"I am just now on my way," I replied. "I just stopped—"

"To see what you could come up with?" His narrow face was eager and drawn, every feature mobile. I pictured his mind to be a scene of windmills, each going a different direction as he worked up a frenzy of alternatives and elaborations. As I ran, all was silent behind me. He had not moved.

❧

It wasn't a lie about the Girl Scout Cookies. I had been putting off the task for weeks, not wanting to go to the blocks in my own zone, and not being allowed to go further, where there lay the delicious possibility of not knowing anyone. At last I had been granted permission to go five blocks past California, and work my way back.

Saturday morning arrived, and having permission, I found that I had no desire. Sunlight lay in hot stripes across my bed. A crow cawed in the Clarks' live oak and somewhere, down toward George's house, a sprinkler spat in paralyzingly even rhythms. The rest of the world was silent, as though in the night everyone had been taken away, leaving me the sole inheritor of a bright, soundless world. Everyone had gone away, but not without raising my window shade high enough so that when I awoke, I would see the fiery leaves of the live oak, and the sky an aching distance behind it, a blue forever receding from my touch. Somehow, it seemed my mother's doing. I dressed slowly, dawdling in the hope that George would appear at my window, and beg to come along on my route.

No one came, and I was forced to walk alone to Andover Street, where the houses sat white and pillared and lost in the midst of enormous lawns. As I walked, I remembered a word my mother had used recently on me. The word was *oblivious,* and though her tone was not complimentary, the word aroused in me a delicious fear, one that suited the houses on Andover Street. In such houses, little girls were kept in shuttered back rooms until their parents wept and repented and admitted their mistakes, and even then, the little girls might not come out. *Oblivious* scooped out a great cavity in my chest, bringing to mind violent scenes in which I was swept into one of these unknown houses by a tall woman with red fingernails and kept prisoner for years, never growing older. No one would know how nearby I was, how I knew everything that went on with them. My parents would go gray with grief and self-recrimination, and George would never marry.

Yet as I advanced upon the wide stone walks of Andover, I had the uncomfortable sensation that George was watching me, and that I looked small and ridiculous. As I walked, this sensation increased, and I decided that once inside the entry of each house, I would ask the owner important questions, perhaps learning secrets I could later tell George. While the doorbell sounded in faraway rooms, I considered possible questions, but the moment footsteps approached, my mouth dried up and nothing but the key words of my speech remained. Door after door opened, everyone ordered something, door after door closed. Only once did an elegant lady with long nails, her lips downturned and red, look at me with a terrible, cruel expression. It was a look she could not remove from her face, no matter how hard she tried, and I left quickly, wondering who it was she had expected.

I was glad to be back in our neighborhood until I saw someone frozen in a bizarre stance directly across from the Candyman's house. His head jutted forward like a bull's, while his hands dangled limply at his sides. It was a beautiful mixture of supplication and fierce demand, and my heart leaped in a confusing manner. At that moment a tiny girl with brown braids came tearing around the corner, chanting and clapping her hands.

"Make George wake up," she cried, dancing around him. "He says only you can make him wake up." She tugged at his shirttails, which fluttered like rags on a scarecrow, though George's face and neck were scarlet. I was moved by his display until the child came up to me. "He says to tell you he won't unfreeze until you sell Girl Scout Cookies to the Candyman," she said.

"I'm doing it anyway," I said. I remembered a line of my mother's. "As far as I'm concerned," I said, "you can stay there until hell freezes over."

No one shouted *Stop, I didn't mean it*, and soon I stood upon a hairy brown welcome mat, gazing up at a pair of gold lions holding between them a small glass lens. The doorbell, when I pressed it, sounded shallowly inside the house. There was a silence so long I began to wish for the whirr of the electric wheelchair. There came a paper-soft sound that might have been slippered feet, then nothing. My eyes stung. I pressed the bell again.

"Lotte," cried a small voice. "Is that you already?"

"It's a little girl," I said. "From Troop Number Three Sixty-five."

"A minute please, a minute."

The gold lions stood upright, face to face, their teeth bared and claws upraised to hold the little lens forever. They looked tired of their pose, as if one of them might without warning drop on all fours and say to the other, "Let's beat it." With a long scrape and clank, the doorchain swung loose, and there was the purple darkness I had expected, in a hallway that smelled not at all dank, but powerfully familiar. In it stood a person no taller than myself, with white hair and the thinnest wrists I had ever seen. Her dress of pale fuzzy wool clung to small hips and small low breasts as though it had been created on her at birth. She peered behind me into the street and I blushed.

"Hello," I said. "My name is Jenny Dietz and I am from Troop Three Hundred and Sixty-five. Your choices are Minty Mint, Vanilla Creme, and Savannah, which is peanut butter with a—"

"I bought already from the other little girl," said the woman. "But you should come in a minute. Come in." She took delicate backward steps into the dark hall as if playing the game "Mother May I." "Shoosh!" she muttered, "I can't see to find them." She stooped over a high-legged table, her legs not bending at all. In the swimming dark of the hall, one of her legs seemed stained a purplish-gray.

"Don't you want another box?" I asked.

"There is no need to be polite with old Mrs. Gadstein," she said. "Save it for a richer customer and let me get a good look at you." She unbent herself, placing on her nose a pair of glasses whose thick lenses made her eyes enormous violet pools. "What's funny," she said, "is that with the other little girl I was so discomboobled that I bought ten boxes of the peanut butter kind, thinking how much Leo would love them." She paused. "I myself have never cared for peanut butter, and now they're sitting. But I am a terrible hostess. Sit down and let me get you a nice glass of lemonade, complete with sliced lemon."

"Oh," I said, "I can't stay—"

But she was gone, taking tiny, stiff steps down a long hallway, her hand raised slightly above a ballet bar like a tightrope walker. I walked through an archway into the front room, as far as possible from the closed door on the other side of the hall.

Along one wall of the living room was a pale blue brocade sofa and a glass coffee table upon which stood a photograph of a soldier, and a black lacquered box. I pressed the button on its lid and immediately eight doors opened, all of them mirrored inside and reflecting beautiful-smelling cigarettes. A song played that I did not know, though it sounded faintly like records my mother played after dinner and which my father called "high class stuff from your mother's side of the family." I looked around for the wheelchair, but there was only a black leather lazy-boy and an ottoman. These took up a whole corner of the dainty blue room.

"Mozart," said Mrs. Gadstein, appearing from nowhere. "Leo picked that up for me in Salzburg many years ago. I myself will not set foot in Europe again." Raising her eyebrows questioningly at me, she handed over a glass, a perfect round of lemon straddling its frosted rim. She went to the ottoman and began to pluck it as if it were a stringed instrument. "Seven years, both of them," she said, "and still I can't get the dog hair off. Between the two of them, I think it was a conspiracy."

There was nothing to hang on to in what she said. "Is Leo the Candyman?" I whispered, already imagining the moment I would tell George what she said. It was difficult to pay attention, thinking how I might present the scene later.

Mrs. Gadstein frowned, still plucking the ottoman.

"Bonbon man," she said. "Bonbon man is better, don't you think?"

Her voice was so quiet, and the room so dim, that I wondered suddenly if hours had passed since I came in. I tried to stand up from the sofa.

"Don't rush off," she said. "It means the same thing, though you should know it first belonged to my father. He was famous in our town for carrying sweets—bonbons—in his pockets for the children. His coats were in ruins five minutes after they came from the wash, what with the bonbons melting and the children hanging from his sleeves like grapes. It drove Mama crazy, but what can you do? He was beloved. Beloved."

Mrs. Gadstein blinked, while nothing else in her face

moved. Her face was a theater mask painted white with pink cheeks and red lips, the eyebrows still upraised and the mouth ready to turn down at any moment, like the mouth of the lady on Andover Street.

"You mean Leo isn't the original Candyman?"

"Who can say?" said Mrs. Gadstein. "Who can say what is original? He had more ideals than a dog has bones, buried. He wanted to be just like my father, only he had the additional idea of being the knight in the old story, who rescues the princess." She gazed toward the hallway and the closed door, her eyebrows rising a notch higher. I sat up straight and gazed with her across the room, which was certainly getting darker. The drapes were closed tight: no light got through, not even a bright sliver full of dust motes that you could push with your hand on a summer morning. George would by now have given me up for dead and gone home with the gruesome tale of my disappearance. Everyone would be sitting down to dinner in lit houses, for certainly every other house in our neighborhood would be lit up. Tears rose to my eyes. Only *I* knew where I was.

"My mother will be worried," I said.

"You're in a rush," she said. "I was selfish to keep you so long. Lotte will be here any minute, of course, probably it is nothing, and you can go home." She stopped and pursed her lips. "I am a terrible hostess. Come into the kitchen for a tiny minute. I have something for you to take home."

"For me?"

"For whom else?" she replied, her face crinkling into thousands of lines. "One of them—I can't remember now if it was Papa or Leo—used to say you should live your life every day as if you were expecting a neighbor to drop in." She rose from the ottoman and walked toward the ballet bar. "It's a nice theory, don't you think?"

)

There was more light in the kitchen, but no clock anywhere. On a table, rows of cards had been laid out for solitaire, and beside them was a plate festively covered by a blue paper napkin—covered completely, as if to intrigue, to drive me crazy. Beyond the window over the sink an enormous tree loomed heavily over two houses, already beginning to lose its definition in the fading light.

"She doesn't know where I am," I said.

"Nonsense," said Mrs. Gadstein. "She is at this very moment pleased that you are paying a call to Vera Gadstein."

The familiarity in her tone startled me. "You know us?" I asked.

She dipped her head gracefully, but whether to affirm or deny I couldn't tell. "You are, what, eleven last June?"

I had to nod.

"One piece of advice," she said. "Don't decide whom you will marry tomorrow. And after you are absolutely positive, wait two weeks. This is advice your mother would be pleased I should give you."

I was going to faint in the dim kitchen. It was as if she had been watching me all along, and was now pulling me under water with my own secret thoughts, letting me up for air only to confuse their meaning, turn everything over and plunge me down again.

"Another secret," she said. "I used to be famous in the

kitchen. I made caramel apples, popcorn balls, you name it. Then Leo took over in the kitchen. 'Sugar,' he said to me. 'Let me do these things for you. Let me wait on you.' It is only now, may he rest in peace, that I have found my kitchen again." She lifted the blue napkin with slow, meticulous tenderness, revealing two round, pale golden cookies crowned with sugar. "My mother's recipe, from when I was your age. I had it by heart as a child and all the time, I never forgot it. I used to recite it to the little ones on our block. They made a song out of it, how did it go?"

The word *block* caught my attention. I looked hard at her. "You mean our block?" I asked. "You mean the little girls who came on Halloween? Was there more than one?" A shiver ran through me. I saw them filing in, one by one, through the dark entry.

She sighed. "There were many, many little girls," she said. Her eyelids drooped like the pink lids of seashells, and the curve of her nose, too, was pink. It twitched once, marionette-like, and I guessed the truth—that against her will the Candyman had led child after child into her house, never letting any of them go.

"You asked a question," she said suddenly. "I am so sorry."

"Never mind," I said. "I better go—"

"Ah!" she said. "I know. You wanted to know about my poor Leo, who wanted to be the Bonbon man."

"Isn't he?" I whispered.

She shrugged noncommittally. "Sometimes I think I am going to open the bedroom door and there he'll be. 'Sweetie-pie,' he'll say. 'Sug, what I could really use is a glass of water,

or even a nice cup of tea—' " She waved her hand in the
air. "I shouldn't speak in vain of him. He meant so well. Certain things I will never forget. How at the very beginning
he wanted to know everything. My name, and the name
of my family, what town I was from, what its population
had been—"

She reached across the table and took my hand. "All I
could remember was the little story about Papa handing out
sweets among the children, and Gadstein, Gadstein, my
mother's maiden name. When I told Leo this, his eyes filled
with tears, as if I told him something important for the whole
world.

"Two days. Two days outside the gates. I looked terrible,
the scar from the fire the least of it, the least, and right there
he asked me to marry him. 'You're a gentile,' I told him, my
heart breaking in half he was so slim and handsome in his
uniform. 'Not anymore,' he said. 'From now on I am Leo
Gadstein and you are my little girl. I want to be your—Bonbon man.' His pronunciation was terrible.

"He was full of fine plans," she continued. "California
was first, even though I told him I had heard they didn't have
seasons there. He was going to buy a boat and teach me how
to sail. And this neighborhood he chose because there were so
many children. He said it was the next best thing, and in
theory, of course, he was right."

"Children did come on Halloween," I said.

"The first year," she said. She flattened her fingers on the
tablecloth and on her hand a diamond ring crouched like a tiny
silver spider on high prongs. "You can eat the cookie now, if
you want," she said.

"Keep telling," I said.

"What's to tell?" she replied. "I was very silly, very child-ish. I wasn't well yet, you know, and when I saw them all filing in, with their little masks, one behind the next so solemn and trusting, and Leo holding out the tray—" She stopped and put her head in her hands. She sat this way, perfectly still, until I could no longer make out the texture of her skin or her hair, but see only a dark head against a brilliant pink sky, and the tree, like a larger, darker head, towering over hers.

"Oh where can Lotte be?" she cried suddenly, gasping for air. "She should have been here hours ago. What if something has happened to her at the bus stop? It is not a safe place where she lives, this Watts."

"Do you want me to call someone?" I asked, standing up.

She nodded, pointing to a little book on the kitchen counter. "Under Johnson," she said.

The name, when I saw it all together, stood out, and I knew why Mrs. Gadstein's hallway smelled familiar. It was the smell of the disinfectant Lotte Johnson swore by.

"Lotte comes to our house, too," I said. "She helps my mother on Thursdays."

"Of course she does," said Mrs. Gadstein. "Your mother sent her to me."

Lotte mopped, dusted, vacuumed with a vengeance. She believed that the man on the moon was a giant television hoax and that it was a sin against God to let a man walk casually through space. Her favorite thing was to shake her finger at me and say, "Your mother has the finest judgment in the world. Etch that on your runaway brain and don't forget it." She had never mentioned the Candyman's wife. All the time she walked through our house she had, somewhere inside of her, the brocade sofa and the lacquered box, and Mrs. Gadstein's voice talking about blocks and towns and fires and handsome soldiers in a way that left something yet untold. I saw Lotte dusting Mrs. Gadstein's hall table, lifting up the thick-lensed glasses and setting them down again. Then, with the same cloth, she would dust our own hall table, while my mother leaned into the refrigerator and said to me, "Jenny, stop with the questions a minute and help me with this salad." In both of their bodies, in their wrists and arms and breasts, lay this knowledge about the insides of other people's houses. A wave of panic flowed through me at the thought of coming home through the dusk to see my parents together in the kitchen, saying things I might never hear about.

"I have to go," I cried.

"Dear me," said Mrs. Gadstein, rising from the table in a single deft motion. She stood still against the sunset, her head, like mine, barely reaching the window ledge, and her features obscured by the violent glow behind her. She turned toward the window. "One thing I have learned," she said, "is that even in Los Angeles there are seasons. A sky like this means autumn is coming. So we will once again have our little autumn."

As she spoke, the streaky light deepened, and the branches of the big tree, which I now knew to be the Clarks' live oak, were not branches anymore, but something utterly new: pure black lace like a Spanish lady's mantilla, floating above a fire. The sky was so bright that I imagined, if she and I were just tall enough, we could peek over the sill and see, spread out at our feet, a whole city on fire, all the buildings and trees silhouetted black in front of flames that never finished devouring them, and in which all of us walked every day, without realizing it. Mrs. Gadstein led me to the front door, finding her way expertly in the dark. She stopped on the threshold as I stepped out onto the flagstone path.

"I'm sorry," she said. "I kept you so long your little friend gave up his pose and went home." Something in her tone suggested she was not sorry at all. She sighed. "Of course, tomorrow he will want an explanation, and you will have to decide what you will and will not tell him."

She took my hand and placed in it something delicate and weighty. It took me a moment to realize it was the cookies, wrapped in their blue paper napkin.

"Give my best to your mother," she said, and her voice floated out like a last, fragile gift on the evening air.

The Beautiful Amelia

Stephen used to catch me worrying at the bathroom mirror. "What do you want to be beautiful for," he'd say. "You've got work to do." But for a long time, I thought it wouldn't be such a terrible thing. Especially if beauty wasn't the tall, blond model with long teeth, short nose, and the knowledge of proper mascara application, but the frail, the luminous, the pale wrist and enormous eyes always gazing after something unreachable, as if lamenting a great loss. It was this quality of Amelia's—unasked for, unworked for, suggesting a mystery beyond all talent—that nearly convinced me I was missing something essential to a real artist's life.

I applied to Castlebrook during my third year at the conservatory, and when I was accepted, I told the whole world. It was reputed to be the best summer music camp in the country. The Boston Symphony performed there every Friday night, and if you played your cards right, you might make valuable connections. Only Stephen pronounced its name with bitterness. Bitterness was his natural talent. He had spent twenty-six years perfecting this and the French horn, and women loved him for it. He scorned the scholarship office and insisted on running around the city in a denim cap muttering to himself. He ate cheap white bread, lived in a stuffy apartment in the Haight, and knew that his suffering made him handsome. The night before I left for Castlebrook he took me to see *Les Enfants du Paradis* for the sixth time. Halfway through, he grasped my arm. I had been waiting over six months for him to kiss me, and leaned to-ward him slightly.

"Carrie," he whispered. "If you're going to have an affair up there, have it with somebody famous." He stood up and walked out of the theater, leaving me to compose seven brilliant responses in his absence.

I was still thinking about his remark when I got on the plane the next morning, taking a window seat beside a middle-aged gentleman who cleared his throat each time I looked up. Holding the demo-tape of "Street Music" in my lap, I tried to regain the feeling of purity I had experienced upon acceptance. Politics, affairs; sure they existed, but they had nothing to do with me. I would be on my guard against corruption from the moment I arrived. Nothing would touch me. I would not go out of my way to speak to famous conductors, except maybe Randolph Martin. He had been the grand old man of Castlebrook for fifteen years. In all the brochure photographs he wore the same remote, stern expression. His dark eyes seemed to say, *I have the secret of playing Chopin.* It was said that as a young man, he forced himself to play straight through the longest, most complicated pieces, not laboring over the troublesome parts until the final practice days. This radical method preserved the unity of the piece from the first moment, and made him famous. He began composing early, terrible things no one would perform. Now, "City Symphonettes" ranked among the great fusions of classical and jazz. He would understand me. He would listen to "Street Music" and sigh. "You're on to something," he'd say. "Don't despair. It reminds me of my own—"

The gentleman beside me cleared his throat. A stewardess was holding a tray precariously over his lap and looking at me.

"Oh, sorry," I said.

"So, you eat," said the man. "You are going home from school?"

"Music camp," I said. "Going, not coming back."

"Ah." He put down his fork. "What instrument?"

"Piano, composition."

He held out a square, pink palm. "Hermann Muller. A pleasure to meet a young musician."

"Carrie Horwicz," I said.

"Horowitz!" he cried. "Related to Vladimir?"

"Not that we know," I said.

"Ach, well," he said. "You never know with immigration." He unwrapped his sandwich delicately, his large fingers plucking at the cellophane. "I must ask," he went on. "You remind me so much of my little grand-niece. You are fifteen, sixteen? So young to travel alone."

"Twenty-two," I said, leaning back against the seat. Randolph Martin would think I was fifteen. He would hand back the tape of "Street Music" and say, "A bit premature. Give it ten years."

Mr. Muller seemed to sense his mistake. "After all," he said. "Mozart looked young for his age."

)

During the bus ride, I tried to concentrate on the beauty of the landscape: something that doesn't come exactly naturally to me. The mountains were not "White" as the name promised, but covered so thickly by pine they seemed impenetrable. No small streams broke the monotony of green ridges, nothing gave the eye access. Thunderheads heaped up with heavy authority, and tall grass of a violent green grew along the road: the sort of grass that has always been my enemy.

I had been wise and taken my allergy shots in San Francisco. I had bought books on the White Mountains and bragged about their beauty to Stephen. "Carrie Horwicz, famed nature lover," he'd said. "Remember Italy? You said you never wanted to see another tree in your life. Face it, Carrie, you and I were meant for the city." He made it sound as if the city was going to digest us, and he was glad. As the bus strained up the mountainside, I realized he was trying to keep me from being inspired without him. Castlebrook's brochures showed students walking in pairs along forest paths, a girl playing a flute in a meadow. With allergy shots, I, too, could be pictured this way. After practice I would walk alone in the woods, purging "Street Music" of its self-conscious moments. If I looked remote and disinterested and did not sneeze, people would come to me. Randolph Martin, walking alone in the opposite direction, would stop and ask to see the notebook in my hands. I would keep it with me at all times.

The air grew still. Thunder cracked overhead like deep,

monstrous timpani. I got out my notebook. What if "Street Music" started like that, with distant drums, *then* the violins. Opening with violins was weak, predictable. A muscular young man jogged past the bus, waving to the driver. As I looked out at him, the driver called out "Castlebrook." Rain had begun to fall, and as I got my suitcase and hauled it to the big building, drops stung my face with increasing rapidity. I pushed open the door and stood a minute, dripping on the carpet.

"Welcome!" said a woman at a long desk. Behind her, a group of people sat before a fire, talking intently. From another room came a pure, flawless fragment of a clarinet solo. I wished I were back in the city.

"Carrie Horwicz," I said.

"Good," said the woman, handing me an envelope. "Here's your packet—you're in the group doing the 'Archduke' trio. Rehearsals start tomorrow in the Annex. We'll tell you more tonight at orientation. If you want to put something in for the composition competition, have it in to me by tomorrow night. You're in Birch, second dorm to the left, room number seven. I believe your roommate just got in. Amelia Albeniz, from Connecticut."

By the time I reached the dorm I was soaked. I walked down the hallway trying not to listen to the conversations in the rooms. Young women laughed and whispered as if they had known each other years, nodding briefly as I passed their doors.

In number seven someone was sitting on one of the two cots. She was pale and disheveled, dressed for a summer day in a flowered dress and sandals.

"Hi," she said. "I think I wore the wrong thing."

"It's hard to know," I mumbled.

"Well," she said, smoothing the bedspread. A flute case rested on it. She touched it lightly, then lifted her hand. "God, I hate being new," she said suddenly. "Do you want to walk around?"

"Yes," I said, glad I didn't have to try out my remote image just yet. I sat down on the other cot and waited while she changed into her jeans.

It turned out she came from a small farm in Connecticut; the name Albeniz went back to a Castilian nobleman in twelfth-century Spain. There wasn't much of the Spanish left in her, she said, sighing, but I thought I saw it. She had a small face and large, olive-colored eyes shadowed delicately beneath, enough to make you wonder what she lost sleep over. She had taken no time with her clothing or hair, yet she gave an impression of sophistication. It was careless, like a natural gift the owner has ceased to value. As we walked about the Castlebrook grounds, she kicked at wet stones with the toe of her sneaker, and talked about how she hated new places, where, she said, everyone was waiting for you to trip and break your neck, and not just metaphorically, either. I could not imagine her falling down in any way; she was utterly free of clumsiness and confusion. Maybe it came from the faint shadows under her eyes, or the smile, a little exhausted. She stirred in me the spontaneous desire to worship. Old, royal blood, I decided. The family tree had never been a popular subject in my family; we came from a hopelessly crude mix of eastern European peasant stock, and our knowledge of famous ancestors stopped abruptly in 1820 with a Hungarian horse thief.

"I almost didn't come," Amelia said. Her tone surprised me; it had the quick, cynical bite of Stephen's voice. "I read an article that said Castlebrook had gone downhill, that politics had taken over. Somebody said that if you sleep with Randolph Martin he'll get you a fellowship at Curtis."

"Maybe somebody else," I said, "not Randolph Martin. He's got no time for that kind of thing. Besides, he's ancient. Who would want to—"

Amelia cocked her head to one side. "Oh, somebody," she said. "It's inevitable."

"Well, if that's what it takes, who wants it?"

She laughed. "Miss Innocence. I'll bet you have a boyfriend."

We were walking toward a big, barnlike building, from which came the sounds of several voices. My nose began to tickle. I tried to ignore it; it seemed impossible, after all the shots. "I don't know what he is," I said. "He pisses me off."

"I'll bet he's nice," said Amelia.

"I don't know," I said. "Can a skinny Jewish man be nice?"

"Yes," she said. "You're in a bad mood."

"Me? No. What about you? I mean, do you have somebody?"

"No." She kicked at the wet stones on the path, and took a deep breath. "Let's go in there."

"I get it," I said. "You just broke up with him." My nose was getting worse, and I didn't have any tissues.

"No," she said. "I didn't just break up with one." She looked at me. "Have you ever been to Florence?"

"Yes. Two summers ago, for the *Maggio Musicale*. I had

hay fever and missed a lot of it. Why?"

"No reason," she said. "I just wish I was there, right now."

"You left a man in Italy," I said.

She wasn't listening. She had opened the big wooden doors and was peering inside. "I think this is the social hall. Want to try it?"

"Not really," I said. "I think my allergies are coming back."

"Come on. You'll feel better inside."

The great smoky hall looked like a hunting lodge. Men stood about in small clusters. As we passed each cluster, it fell silent.

"What happened to the women?" I whispered.

"They're in the dorm, gossiping," said Amelia, leading me toward the fireplace at the far end. Two men sat before it, and as we approached, they stopped talking. One of them, a tall, blond, ranch-hand sort of man, stood up.

"I'll get some chairs," he said, looking at Amelia.

"No thanks," she answered. "We'd rather stand. I'm Amelia Albeniz, and this is Carrie, um—"

"Horwicz," I said.

"Amelia Albeniz," said the tall man. "What a beautiful name. Spanish?"

"Way back," she answered.

The other man and I stared into the fire. I felt the bottoms of my pockets for a stray tissue. Nothing.

"Related to Vladimir?" he asked.

"Distantly," I said. I knew I should ask his name, and what instrument he played, but the tickling in my nose had increased. "Excuse me a second," I said.

"Carrie," cried Amelia. "Don't leave."

I waved her away and turned. It was too late. For a quarter of a second, pure bliss, then I opened my eyes to see the seated man wiping his jeans with small, polite movements.

"I'm so sorry," I said. "Excuse me."

"I'll come with you," said Amelia. She seemed in a hurry to get out of there.

❯

The only places I felt safe were the piano cells and the rehearsal room. The infirmary's little yellow pills made me sleepy, so I gave up on the nature walk idea. I didn't mind, really: "Archduke" rehearsals took all morning; it was a lovely time. The three of us drank our coffee and started right in; our performance was in two weeks. It always surprised me when Amelia appeared in the doorway a few minutes before lunch. She had already taken her flute back to the room, but still carried a folder of music under one arm. She stood in the doorway watching us intently, as if trying to pick out one part from the rest. Her attention confused and flattered me. I remained flattered until we entered the dining hall. The moment we chose our table, men rushed to fill the seats around Amelia. Tom the ranch-hand was always there. He brought his friend Jeffrey, and then fell into a desperate, hunched concentration, like a craftsman working over a piece of beautiful broken china. One day, as an experiment, I ventured a remark. No one heard it. I tried another, and Tom nodded responsively to Amelia. After lunch, he invited her to take a walk.

"Only if Carrie comes," she said.

"Can't," I said. "Got to practice."

"Of course," said Tom. He nudged Jeffrey, who was gazing thoughtfully at his plate, and they left.

As soon as they were gone, another young man approached Amelia and suggested a walk.

"Sounds nice," she said.

I looked at her in awe.

"I just met him today," she said. "He didn't give me
a line."

My special route to the piano cells was a big loop around
the meadow. It wasn't good for my nose, but I had to do it, for
this was where Randolph Martin took his daily constitutional.
After lunch he marched around the field in white duck trousers and a long denim coat. His white hair stood straight up
in an outgrown military crew cut, and from a distance, you
could see his head wag a little as he walked. A few times I had
come within nodding distance of him, but this time I was
certain he had inclined his head. I ran to my cell and closed
the door behind me. It was entirely possible that he had had
a chance to look over the competition tapes, and that the incli-
nation of his head was a secret sign to me. I gazed up at the
tiny cell window, up into the burning leaves, the branches
knocking against the glass. Amelia was at this very moment
walking through the woods with a handsome young man who
stared at her as she stared elsewhere. But wasn't the inclined
head of Randolph Martin better than a thousand stricken
young men? I sat down at the piano and attacked the "Archduke" as if it were a secret and potent enemy.

The next day Amelia rushed up to me in the lunch line
with the news that Randolph Martin wanted to join us for
lunch.

"Why not?" I said, coolly taking three pieces of bread for my sandwich.

We took our seats and shooed away four young men, including Tom, who shot a fierce, animal glance in my direction. At last, Randolph Martin arrived. With a single grave and deliberate movement, he set his tray down opposite Amelia. Up close his eyes were slightly bloodshot. His great jowls fluttered as he prepared to speak.

"Hello, girls," he said.

"I'm Carrie," I said. "Carrie Horwicz."

His eyes rested on my face for one exquisite moment. His gaze was comfortable, as if I were a child who had pleased him with some little attention. Then he turned to Amelia.

"And you are Amelia Albeniz," he said. His eyes grew watery, and into his face came the strained, eager look I had come to recognize all over Castlebrook. "They tell me you went to Curtis."

"Only for summer classes," she said.

He reached across the table and patted her hand. "I always take a walk with my Curtis girls," he said. "After lunch, shall we?"

"Carrie?" asked Amelia.

"Got to practice," I said. I finished eating and dashed out. I passed the practice rooms and walked into the woods, clutching a tissue in my pocket. The pines towered over me, throwing shadows on the narrow path, shutting out the sunlight. At this moment, Amelia and Randolph Martin would reach the duck pond. Amelia would toss pebbles into the water and Randolph Martin, looking at her beautiful pale hands, would inquire what instrument she played. Finally I turned back to the cells. Someone was calling me. Amelia and Randolph Martin stood in the great meadow, beckoning.

"Can't," I cried, tapping my nose.

)

If Randolph Martin did not eat at our table, he took Amelia to another. Each day after lunch, she accompanied him on his walk. I took the short route to the cells. One night, Amelia asked me what was wrong.

"Carrie," she said. "You're such a snob. Randolph thinks you hate him."

"First-name basis," I muttered.

"It's no big deal. We're friends."

"That's good. Then you don't need a chaperone."

I went to lunch with the violinist and cellist of the "Archduke" group. I found that as long as I stayed away from Amelia at social gatherings, I was visible, maybe even likable. It was slow work, though. There were days when my only goal was to get to the cell without having to speak to anyone. I wore my most faded jeans and carried a book to all lectures and concerts so my solitude would appear self-imposed.

By the first Boston Symphony concert my misery had risen to such a pitch that it was no longer romantic. As luck would have it, the last piece was Albinoni's "Adagio," which breaks your heart even when you've heard it fifty times. I was sitting in the back, with a perfect view of the quivering white head of Randolph Martin four rows down, leaning toward the smaller, brown one of Amelia. I counted the beats in each measure to steady myself, but it was no use. The violins come in on the ninth, and it hurts, no matter what you do. Knowing that the manuscript was found in the ruins of a Dresden attic after World War II hurts, too; it fits the lonely, low plucking of the cellos, the waiting for the next instrument. It could have been lost; the whole business of discovery is so fragile. I didn't bother with tissues. I held my head up and listened, thinking how, if Stephen were here, he would, at the most melting moment, hold his dirty sleeve up to my face and say, "Wipe on here if you need to."

When it was over I ran out of the hall and into the wide valley night. Groups emerged slowly and stood about the lawn talking quietly. Tom the ranch-hand stood alone, looking all around. I started toward him just as another girl walked up and touched his arm. I left the lawn and headed toward the dark dormitory.

Inside the room I closed the door and switched on the desk lamp. On the desk lay a half-finished letter to Stephen, full of breezy remarks about the "Archduke's" "executioners." I sat down and wrote two pages of uninhibited self-pity, read it over and tore it up. The door opened, and a pale, stern Amelia walked in.

"I'm depressed," she said, dropping onto her cot.

I didn't answer.

"Carrie?"

"You have no right to be depressed," I said. "You have two hundred men in love with you, and Randolph Martin asked you to call him by his first name. What more do you want?"

"I don't know," she said. "Sometimes I wish I were you. When you get a compliment, you know they mean it. You work for it."

"Thank you," I said.

She stared down at the bedspread. She looked the way she had on the first day, before I found out she was beautiful: pale, a little chilled, nervous. "It doesn't matter," she said. "Nobody wants me to actually *accomplish* something—" She plucked at the bedspread, then stood up abruptly. "I knew I was going to get depressed up here." She walked to the bureau and from the bottom drawer brought out a bottle of Jack Daniels. "Want some?" she asked, holding up two tea cups.

"Whiskey doesn't seem like your drink," I said.

"If we get drunk enough we can crash the faculty party."

"Maybe," I said. I thought if I could get her talking she'd forget about the party. "So, you never told me about Italy."

"Oh, it was typical."

"No," I said.

She nodded and swallowed her whiskey. I pictured the whole thing, the grotesque misunderstanding; the man very slim, stumbling into English beautifully, his dark hair thinning just enough to keep his handsomeness intelligent. He was looking away from Amelia so that she wouldn't see how in love he was, and she, of course, took this as a sign of rejection.

"It was no big deal," she said.

But I knew it was. It was this experience in Italy which made her so sad, this which kept her voice calm and distant in the treacherous present. Whatever had happened with the slim Italian, it had tragic proportions, and Amelia was trying to deny them. I looked at her dark, shapely head, at her eyes, which under the lamplight looked more stunned, more vulnerable than ever, and a sense of utter defeat shot through me. Nothing so mysterious had happened to me; I would never look that way. My own Italy was blurred by sneezes, by great heaps of tissue. I had met Stephen on that trip, and he had accompanied me to all the pharmacies, pointed to my swollen face while I sneezed on command. The difficulty was finding something that wouldn't put me to sleep. Stephen danced around the druggists, imitating insomniacs and pianists and shouting, "Awake! Awake!" One afternoon he made me lie down in the pensione while he went to another pharmacy. He lay wet paper towels tenderly over my face and said, "Don't move." He left. I knew that outside my window there was soft sunlight, dusty pink stucco, ladies hanging their wash over the courtyard. Water splashed over cobbles from a high-up window, and on another street, a band played a terrible march. Summer ran through everything; even the motorbikes rushing past seemed less raucous. When Stephen came back I was standing at the desk. He had a small bottle in his hand.

"You're supposed to keep them shut!"

"In a minute," I said. I wrote down everything I could, beginning pianissimo with a single, atonal string of notes on violin, then a second violin following. Gradually the two growing louder and resolving into a melodic duet.

"Here's your medicine."

I wanted to tell him all about it, but I was afraid he would tell me it was only delirium from my allergies. Even later, back home, I was afraid that was what it was. I didn't leave Florence transformed like Amelia; maybe something had happened to me, but it didn't give me mystery. I wondered what it felt like to be such a person. Under the spell of the whiskey and the privacy of our small room I tossed my head dramatically. Amelia seemed to awaken from a trance.

"He liked me, I think," she said. "We kept meeting at this café. He never gave me a line, he was very quiet about himself. No one had ever asked me so many questions. I felt like a person with something to say. Every morning we drank our coffee, and he stood up to leave, raising his hands in this funny reluctant way he had."

"How did he mess it up?" I asked.

"It wasn't him," she said sharply, as if I'd trampled on sacred ground. "I was curious about his life, he said so little. One morning I followed him up the hill, and looked in through the lattice-work at a garden so green, so private, I'm still not sure I didn't make it up. But I remember I didn't want anything more from life at that moment, I was glad to be outside, looking in. He came out into the garden and stood in an archway, looking right at me. I didn't move, I knew he couldn't be really seeing me."

"But he was," I said, utterly despondent. It was so utterly Amelia, all that delicate, cinematic denial.

"No. I heard the creak of a chair, and right in front of me a young man stood up and stretched like a cat. I was completely invisible, I didn't exist. I ran as fast as I could downhill. I didn't want to see how happy they were.

"The next day when he came for coffee, he said 'There's someone I'd like you to meet.' I cut him off, I said I wasn't interested. I left Florence the next day."

"Why?" I said. "Maybe he was just a friend, or a brother, maybe he wanted you to meet the family."

"Don't be naive," she said, laughing a little. "I knew right from the start he had somebody else; that's why I fell in love with him. Nice and unattainable."

I was stunned. With one swipe she had knocked away my pleasant vision of her Florence: the small, steaming cups of espresso, sunlight and tantalizing shyness—I realized I'd been seeing myself at the lattice-work, not Amelia, I hadn't been seeing her at all.

"Come on," she said. "We're drunk enough."

"It's restricted."

"Don't be silly. Nobody's guarding the door. And anyway, Randolph will vouch for us."

"He'll vouch for you," I said.

❭

As we ran across the dark road I decided I would not hunt for people to speak to; I would stand coolly against a wall and wait for them to come to me. When they did, I would gaze out the window and answer no questions I thought were stupid. My head felt pleasantly numb until I remembered that in the morning the competition results would be posted.

"Amelia," I said. "I don't feel well. I'm going back."

"Liar," she replied in the dark. She pulled at my sleeve. "Stop faking."

Eighty people were packed into the small lodge. Faculty members stood surrounded by admirers whose heads jutted eagerly forward, whose drinks tipped precariously toward their mentors' jackets. Someone handed me a beer. I sipped at it continuously as I tried to keep Amelia in my range of vision.

"Where are we going?" I shouted.

"To find Randolph," she said.

"That's crazy. There are other people to talk to."

"I know," she said. "But I promised—"

A young man stood in our path. "Amelia," he said.

"Oh, hi," she said.

I turned away and found myself looking at the throat of Tom the ranch-hand.

"Hello," I said.

"Hi, Carrie."

"Look," I said. "I know you think I'm awful. But I want you to know I wasn't playing chaperone. Amelia—"

"Awful?" he frowned at me. "No, I was going to say I like it a lot. I heard the second section. It's wild."

"What's wild?" I asked. "She's using me as a screen, to keep men away."

"Do you feel all right?" he asked, smiling.

"Thank you," I said. "You're absolutely right." My head burned. I had a sudden vision of Amelia standing in the doorway of our rehearsal room, her fingers tightening around her own music book. I looked around, but she was gone. The young man was talking to somebody else.

"Relax," said Tom. "You're so goddam nervous nobody can talk to you. Where are you from?"

"San Francisco," I said. Behind us, two women were talking about a faculty member. "Tom," I said. "Listen."

"So," said one. "We're talking about Curtis, you know, that's his opening line, and suddenly he puts his hand on my left breast, just like that, and keeps right on talking about the department."

"I love it," said the other.

Tom shook his head. "That's old hat," he said. "You know who."

"No," I said.

"He's famous for it. Always goes for the left breast. I wonder if it's something Freudian—"

"Excuse me," I said.

He put his hand on my shoulder. "The bathroom is upstairs. Need assistance?"

"No," I said. "Fresh air, better."

"Come back sometime," he said.

❯

Above the swaying broad backs of the guests I saw the porch, and beyond it, the great meadow. There, I thought, I will not be sick. I will breathe deeply and watch this party from the outside. I stumbled and grasped a man's arm.

"Steady," he said, turning to me. "Why hello. Are you the young lady—"

"No," I said. I pushed forward, finally reaching the screen door. In the dim light I saw the outline of a round table and gripped its edge.

"I was in the forty-second air command," said a deep, quavering voice at my elbow. "We flew over Germany every day; you never knew whether that day you were going to be shot down. I was twenty-two years old, my dear, just your age."

"That's amazing," said a young female voice. "It's so hard to imagine."

In the faint light I made out the large head with its stiff white hair, and close beside it, the smaller, delicate one. Randolph Martin's hands rested on the table.

"Ah, good," I said.

"Carrie, is that you?" called Amelia. "Randolph was just asking about you."

"We've met," I said. "At lunch, I believe."

"Of course," said Randolph. "Please join us."

"Can't, really. I am looking for air."

"You've been very unhappy here, haven't you," he said.

"Me? No, not at all. Who said I was unhappy?"

He laughed. "Well, at any rate, I imagine you feel better now. We are all looking forward to the Friday performance."

"Beethoven's Seventh?" I said.

"Well, yes, that too," he said. "I was thinking of the afternoon, and your charming little piece."

"Carrie," said Amelia. "Why don't you sit down."

"I will," I said. "If you'll go on about the war."

Randolph nodded and began to speak. I missed some things, but I remember the part about the liberation of the camps, how he and his fellow GIs handed out Hershey's chocolate to the prisoners, who wept over the hard, stale pieces. He had never quite recovered from that sight, he said; the war had cured him of his illusions about fame, about what mattered. His head drooped closer to Amelia's, his shoulder touched hers. She flinched only slightly, then relaxed, her shoulders caving in a little. Randolph did not notice. Amelia's face was lost in shadow, her voice a shadow too, as she murmured questions to keep him talking. I saw suddenly the flute case on her cot, her fingers tapping the bedspread on the first day. I had never asked her what group she was in, and when it would perform. Tonight I would see the flute case again, in moonlight on her cot. At what moment had I let her down?

"Excuse me," I said, rising.

"Don't go," cried Amelia. "I want you to hear this."

"I'll come back," I said. "I promise." I turned toward the great meadow that I knew lay just beyond the porch. Along the horizon lay a ridge of the White Mountains: a ghostly, imposing block against the sky. I wanted to run across the meadow to it, up to the foot of the quiet, solemn granite, where I would not be able to hear the quivering disappointment of the famous and the beautiful; where, in the cool, remote presence of stone, I could regain my first vision of them. If I could get there, and back—

The edge of the porch came sooner than I expected. In the air I had time to think, *lovely, weightless,* before a dull thump sounded in my ears. I felt as though I had been wrapped in wet, cold mud.

"Are you all right?" asked Randolph Martin.

I opened my eyes. Through the high, wet web of grasses I could see the sky, crammed with stars, and the figures of Randolph and Amelia bent over me. Up close, their faces wore the look of people awoken abruptly from troubling, early morning dreams: embarrassed, and yet relieved. I knew they were waiting for me to answer them, and I also knew that very soon, I would sneeze and break the spell. Stephen would certainly have laughed, but that was all right. I lay still, picturing everything the way I wanted it, Amelia curled up on her cot, the Friday afternoon performance long, long, past. For a moment, I had things right, and I think they knew it, for neither of them spoke, or moved, or went anywhere else in the world.

Judgment

We once had a housekeeper who seemed to know an important secret. She was the widow Francisca Rodriguez, and when I was eight, I followed her around our house like an unsanctified disciple, hoping to find out what it was. On a chain around her neck she wore a small silver cross, and I was sure this had something to do with her knowledge, because whenever it slipped out of her blouse she held it shyly between her fingers before dropping it back down out of sight. I, too, had a little pendant on a chain—a Star of David—but it meant nothing to me and was, besides, chilly on my collarbone. I could not stop thinking of Mrs. Rodriguez's silver cross lying bright against her skin where nobody could see it.

On Thursdays, when Mrs. Rodriguez came to help my mother, I was to keep out of the way. I was impatient for those particular nights, a Friday or a Saturday, when I had her all to myself. The moment my parents left the house, our ritual began. I wrapped myself in a quilt and pressed my back firmly against the kitchen-closet door so that nothing could escape out of it, while Mrs. Rodriguez locked up the milk-door. Then, her fingers still shy, she unlaced her white oxfords so that I could see again the tiny white lines that criss-crossed her heels from walking barefoot in the California desert. If I was good, she brought out her black shawl and moved her feet in a flat, shuffling pattern I couldn't imitate. In the middle of this dance she might stop suddenly and put her finger to her lips. Folding up her shawl with excruciating slowness, she tucked her shoes under the kitchen table and led me to my room. I went there in delicious fear, for she made me see how dark the world really was: just beyond the streetlights was a landscape of giant, sharp-needled cacti and dark-red mountains named Sangre de Cristo, the blood of Christ. By the way in which she raised her eyebrows as she brought down each window shade, I knew she saw things I couldn't see, and so I ignored her completely when, as she tucked me in, she said, "This is only a story, *muchacha.*" Her eyes were open wide, her hands moving constantly, so that I knew everything she told me was true—that as she spoke, the villagers were gathering around my window for the ceremony; that the scratching sound I heard, like a crow walking on dead leaves, was the old crone of the village, who made sure everything went according to plan. The faint creak—these were the ropes being looped around the wrists and ankles of the chosen young man.

"You must help me tell it," said Mrs. Rodriguez. "If I get a date wrong, or mix up the names, the villagers will leap right through this window and visit such a judgment on me as you and I could not imagine."

She always let me end the story—this was to keep me from having a nightmare afterwards—and I always ended it the same way.

"The young man has a girlfriend," I said, "and late at night when no one is looking she cuts the rope and he gets down off the big sticks and they run away together, and he doesn't die."

"That is a fine ending," said Mrs. Rodriguez. "A nice ending to keep in your mind when you shut your eyes."

Although I tried this, sometimes everything got confused in my dreams, and it was I who cut the ropes and tried to lead the young man away through the mountains in the darkness. Somehow we weren't in the mountains but in my town, walking past my house, and I offered him Cheerios and he wouldn't take any, and when at last I looked up at his face it was hidden in a dark hood, and he refused to let me see him.

My mother stood by my bed, asking me what I had dreamed that made me cry out.

I shook my head. "It's a secret between Mrs. Rodriguez and me," I said.

The next time Mrs. Rodriguez came to stay with me, she would not speak of the *penitentes*.

"They are all gone from the world," she said, "and you are getting the wrong idea of Catholics. We will get permission from your mama to go to the Mission, and there you can see for yourself that we are just like you."

❭

The next Saturday she held my hand firmly. We walked around and around a bright dusty courtyard, scattering bird-

seed in front of the fat pigeons. The edges of the palm trees
hung over us, shining like swords. Deep orange and red blos-
soms clung to the crumbling balconies. At one end of the
courtyard was an open door, dark as the mouth of a cave, with
flies hovering around it. Just before it, an old woman dressed
in black crawled on her knees.

"Don't stare, *muchacha*," said Mrs. Rodriguez. "She is
atoning for something."

"I want to atone," I said. "I want to go in the little closet
and confess."

She laughed at me. "Your God is the same as ours," she
said. "Your parents atone for a whole day in September, and
soon you will, too."

I said this was not true. All we had in our religion was
Friday night, when my mother set out the braided white candles and the purple cup. She lit the candles, passing her hands
in front of her eyes. It was true that something happened in
September, but nobody atoned for anything as far as I could
see, and my mother came away from the synagogue with a
headache. Mrs. Rodriguez sighed when I told her this. "Atoning is hard work," she said. "Sometimes I could do without it
myself."

I did not believe she meant it. She was trying to keep me
away from a dangerous mystery she knew all about. At school,
when we were asked to draw pictures of our houses, I drew
a balcony of red flowers and an arched doorway shaded in a
dark mix of crayon. I gave Mrs. Rodriguez the picture, and
waited for her praise.

"Make a picture for your own mama," she said, frowning.
"Make a picture of your pretty house."

)

September came. I watched my parents closely to see if the prospect of a whole day of atoning moved them. A year of mixed-up dates and forgotten names lay behind them, but they only became solemn, as if readying themselves for the funeral of a distant relative. One night my mother brought out my blue dress with the sailor collar and cuffs. From my bead box she brought out the Star of David.

"I don't want to," I said.

"On the Day of Atonement you will wear your Star of David," she said. "Why should you be the only little girl with nothing on her neck?"

After she listened to me say the *Shema, the Lord our God, the Lord is One,* and kissed me goodnight, I got out of bed and stood by the window, trying not to move or blink. This was how the *penitentes* made themselves sick. I waited for the blinding streaks of light, for the brightness that would illuminate the invisible towering cacti and the red mountains, but the darkness only thinned and drew coolly back, taking away the stars. Hot, then chilled, I went down the hall to my parents' room and lay down before the door. When they found me, the expression on my face would be brave and sad. They would understand that I had been through something more important than High Holiday services and would have to stay with Mrs. Rodriguez while they went to the synagogue.

)

At suppertime the sky was yellow and clear. The kitchen table shone; even the pale blue sprigs of my pajamas had a yellow glow on them. They seemed ready to float upwards into the sky.

All of this went unnoticed by my parents. My father stood at the head of the table, his neck flushed and clean above his dark suit. My mother moved back and forth between us, setting out the *challah*, wine, and chicken. She put a plate before me and without a word lit the two braided candles. She held her hands before her eyes until the little diamond faced the flame and turned yellow, too.

"You put yourself in the dark for a moment," she said to me, "and then suddenly, there's the light, just like the first time." In the candlelight and the flat yellow glow coming through the windows, her shiny black belt and earrings gleamed like licorice, and every hair on her arms was lit bright. My father hummed and cleared his throat and said the blessing over the wine without being asked. When he finished, my mother looked over the candles at him for a long time, and I realized that they, too, had a secret religion—one that had nothing to do with me. They were going to synagogue without me, and it was possible that they would not come back for me afterward, since I had made such a fuss.

In the car, the distance between us was immeasurable. Their clean necks and dark, smooth collars were too high to reach, and even if I could have reached them, I was certain they would not feel my touch. Outside, the lawns and windows of our neighborhood flew backward, taking on a glassy, evacuated look. I longed for someone, anyone, to appear at a window and wave at me as we passed.

We crossed the main boulevard of our town, and our street took on a new name: *Escondido.*

"That's Spanish for *hidden*," said my father, "but there's not much hidden here."

Escondido Street was narrow and lined with tall, emaciated palms that leaned inward toward the road. Each house was perfectly square and painted pink or green: each was sunk at a different angle into a square of crabgrass.

"You're lucky tonight," said my mother. "Mrs. Rodriguez's little niece is staying with her. You'll have a playmate."

In front of the houses children played in their underwear, staring as our car passed. I waited for the ticking of the turn signal, for the car to round a corner and reveal the adobe arch of the Mission, the brilliant flowers hanging down around a doorway. The car moved straight down the street, stopping at last before a signal box that flashed red and clanged.

"This is it," said my father, but no one moved. A train appeared, rumbling past the last house on the street. As it rocketed past, a girl on a rocking horse in the yard rushed toward the tracks as if she meant to throw herself under the wheels. Along with her went something red and fluttery. Whatever it was, it was yanked under the wheels of the train and did not reappear. The girl laughed and clapped her hands.

"That must be Jayanna," said my father.

"Be good," whispered my mother. "You'll be asleep when we come back for you."

)

Jayanna was back on her rocking horse, pitching its nose, then tail, to the grass. As she rocked, her dark tangled hair escaped its elastic band and flowed behind her with a violent life all its own. Her pink shorts glowed in the dusk.

"Doesn't that make you feel sick?" I asked her.

Jayanna pitched forward, standing up. "Sick?" she shouted.

"Doing that," I said.

"Anyway else is for little kids," she said. "Want to try?"

"I would," I said, "only I was sick last night."

"Oh, oh," said Jayanna, stopping her horse. "Now I know who you are. You're the little one my Nana stays with. She said you were real small."

"Nana," I said, looking down at the stiff grass. I wanted to squat down and scratch my toes, concentrate deeply on scratching.

Jayanna smiled. "Nana is my aunt," she said. "What do *you* call her?"

"Oh, it depends," I said. "Sometimes I call her Nana, sometimes Francisca. We tell stories together, and she takes me to the Mission."

"I bet she doesn't take you in the church," said Jayanna.

"Yes, she does," I said. "It's beautiful—all lit up with candles."

"It's not that lit up," she replied. "It's so big it's mostly dark. Sometimes *gringos* fall down when they walk inside, it's so dark."

"I didn't fall down," I said.

"Did you cross yourself?"

I nodded, trembling.

Jayanna closed her eyes. "Once a man came to the Mission, and crossed himself though he wasn't Catholic. You know what happened? The Holy Mother came right off her platform and broke in a million pieces at his feet. He died later." Jayanna opened her eyes wide, as Mrs. Rodriguez did in the *penitente* story. "They aren't just statues," she said. "The Mission is—our sacred place, where the saints live and breathe." She sat back on the horse and drew a deep breath.

"Jayanna!" cried a voice from somewhere in the house. I opened my mouth to cry back *I'm here too*, but Jayanna had already jumped off the horse and gone to stand on the porch. She looked taller than ever, her brown hair falling around her face and her legs planted firmly apart.

By the time I got up there she was tugging on Mrs. Rodriguez's apron. "Can we go to the Mission," she cried, "just for a minute?"

"The church is not a good place for a little one," said Mrs. Rodriguez, looking at me. "By the time we get back it will be pitch-dark."

"Oh," said Jayanna, "it won't hurt her, just for a minute."

"I want to go too," I said.

Mrs. Rodriguez frowned, and drew away from both of us. "We won't stay more than a minute," she said.

When we reached the Mission the sky was flat as a burnished wooden floor. The adobe arches and iron bell of the courtyard stood sharply outlined against it, while our shadows grew faint on the pavements. Halfway across I stopped to let Jayanna and Mrs. Rodriguez walk ahead. I was not Catholic, and I would be struck down for entering the place where the saints lived and breathed. I saw the face of the Holy Mother, her eyelids downcast as she judged the offender and toppled before him. And I knew that Jayanna, standing among the saints, would speak. They would, of course, listen, for she knew something important—I had never before heard anyone so certain of things. As I stood in the courtyard I remembered my father raising the cup of wine and hesitating as he spoke the words of the blessing. I could not keep a picture of him in my mind.

Mrs. Rodriguez was waiting for me at the church door. "It is nothing to be afraid of, *muchacha*," she said. "Just candles and old statues, that is all."

Inside, it smelled like an old enormous closet where costumes are kept. In far corners small red glasses of flame flickered, threatening to go out. They cast a faltering light on the chins and the lowered eyelids of the statues in their alcoves.

"This place is very, very old," said Mrs. Rodriguez. She knelt and moved her hand across her forehead and chest.

I crouched beside her and tried to imitate the gesture.

"You don't need to do that," she whispered, pulling me to my feet.

"How come?" asked Jayanna, kneeling on her other side.

"Because Jewish people have other customs," she said.

Jayanna rose. Her eyes slanted upward to the saints in their alcoves and she opened her mouth.

"Don't!" I cried. Covering my ears with my hands, I ran down the aisle toward the door and the dim blue rectangle of the courtyard. Near the door, my foot touched down on a small pile of black cloth. Out of the corner of the crumpled cloth came a bony hand and a gray head, and the terrible creaking sound of the *penitente*'s ropes. As the old woman crawled past, her hand rose higher and higher, and a bitter, undefinable smell rose up, too. In terror I struck at the hand and ran into the courtyard, hearing, faintly, the sound of Spanish behind me.

❭

No one spoke on the way back. Mrs. Rodriguez walked swiftly, her stride almost military, and we could not keep up. When we reached the yard she held up her hand. "Play together until I call you," she said. We stood still, the rocking horse a dim blue shadow between us, watching as a light went on in each room Mrs. Rodriguez passed through. In the last room she bent over a pink-fringed lamp and sat down in a chair, plucking a pair of knitting needles into a length of wool.

Behind the rocking horse, Jayanna's face was unreadable. I had done something terrible, but though I could still see the church aisle and Jayanna's upturned face, I could not think what it was. After a moment she smiled and crooked her finger. I followed her to the side of the house, my head lowered.

"Don't you hear it?" she whispered.

"What?"

"Listen," she said, "Ah, there he is!" She stooped quickly to the grass and picked something up. "Here, *catch!*" she cried, and something tiny and fluttering landed in my hands. As they closed over it, the fluttering stopped. The thing lay motionless in my palm, a narrow papery length.

"Don't," I cried, "I don't want it." I tossed it back to her and she stepped to one side. The insect fell to the grass between us.

"You held it too hard," she said. "I'm pretty sure you

killed it." She drew her breath in harshly. "I know some-thing," she said. "Sister Marlena told us."

"What?" I said.

"She said, she said . . . that Jesus' blood is on your heads, and that's how come everybody hates—" She stopped and looked at me in a kind of amazement. In the twilight I saw my hand come up from my side and sweep across her face.

"Nana!" she cried. "Oh, oh!"

Mrs. Rodriguez appeared at the back door, the knitting needles still in her hand. She put her arm around Jayanna and led her into the house. When she came back her face was downcast. She would not look into my eyes.

"Come sit with me," she said. She brought me into a room and set books on the floor beside me. Picking up the piece of wool, she sat down and began to work the needles, silently, deftly.

"Is she okay?" I asked.

"Yes," said Mrs. Rodriguez. "You do not hit very hard. But why—"

"Jesus' blood is—is on—" I bent my head over the book. I saw the lowered eyelids of the saints, and felt again the rough papery hand. "Did we do something bad?" I cried.

"No, *muchacha*," she said.

"Can I sleep in your bed tonight?" I asked.

"No," she said. "Jayanna has given you the guest bed. Shall we go now, and be brave?"

）

The room had no boundaries in the dark. There had to be an end to it, I thought, furniture or a back wall. I played that the room was my room at home—if I could see, I would see a rocking chair in one corner, and the shelf of dolls, and the cat clock whose big eyes went back and forth all night. I blinked in the darkness and tasted the salt on my arms for comfort. I pulled the scratchy wool blanket up to my nose and lay down, trying to guess whether my eyes were open or shut. Once a sliver of light appeared beneath the door, and my arms and legs tingled. "Dad?" I cried, but the thin line of light went out. Far away, a car engine grumbled and passed, the slow hum of it echoing in the street.

I was still listening for it when a new, deeper humming began, building until the bed began to shake. I sat up. Intervals of yellow light streamed through the window, lighting up a figure on the floor. Jayanna's face was smooth and unperturbed. Little droplets of perspiration showed on her forehead, and her lips were parted, as if she were having a conversation with someone in her dream.

She did not awaken as a prolonged moan traveled toward us, and the yellow light went red and still. All the objects in the room stood out against the flat surfaces of the walls like mountains on a relief map. Near the door, a small plaster woman ticked toward the edge of a bureau, her eyes closed and her small hands clasped neatly together. The braided rug beneath Jayanna was bathed in red, but still she slept, no trace of my slap on her cheek. I turned away from her and the tiny woman to touch the cool, smooth comfort of the headboard.

It was so small I could not at first make out what it was, and knelt on the bed for a closer look. There, on the headboard, a tiny man hung upon a pair of crossed sticks, his perfect ivory limbs twisted in the wrong directions. On his feet were twin spots of blood, and his head was sunk upon his left shoulder at an unbearable angle. Unlike the woman on the bureau, his eyes were wide open, and gazed into mine with a helpless expression, as if to say that he, too, had been awake all night. He seemed, from that difficult position, to be asking to come down.

Under the doorway the bright light streamed again; I heard my father's voice in the hall, coming toward me. I looked down at Jayanna, but her face had forgotten everything in sleep. She was finished with me.

"Okay, Jesus, you can come down now," I whispered. I reached up, but he was farther away than I thought, and when the door swung open, my hand was caught in the glare of the hall lamp.

Staying Under

We're in Hartford. I've got a window seat all the way to the back, and the minute he steps on I know he's going to sit next to me, out of all the empty seats on that bus. I know the best thing is to slouch down and act interested in the scenery, but there isn't any scenery in Hartford, and the way he holds his duffle, he wants me to look at him. He holds it up high and straight out in front of him so every hard little muscle in his arm stands out.

He's wearing headphones; everybody can hear the tinny *tsch-tsch-tsch* as he comes down the aisle. Nobody turns a head but they're all watching him. That's the bus: when you get on, everybody checks you out without moving their faces at all. They fold their arms and check you out, and if you catch their eye they look at your shoulder, like they're looking through you to something more interesting. Like they figured you out and forgot you before you got by. It used to be hard for me to walk down here to the back, but now I'm different and I don't have to pay attention. I pray for the strength not to look at this guy, but the duffle and the straight arm are right in front of me. I can't help it. I keep my eyes on the duffle and his wrist; I won't look in his eyes, because that's asking for it. I look at the duffle, knowing he's looking at me and waiting. The *tsch-tsch* is right in my ear.

"This taken?" he asks.

I shake my head. I'm strong now; I don't have to say a word. He can sit here if he wants, but he can't get anything out of me if I don't want to. The man up in Maine said if I ever felt afraid I was losing it, I should just touch my fingers to a cross and that would remind me. I do. It's cold between my fingers and cold lying down on my collarbone. It's my first jewelry and it makes me feel undressed.

)

When nobody's next to you, you can be yourself. You can lean the seat back and sit cross-legged if you want, or let them lie open like boys do. Nobody can see. Maybe there's somebody across the aisle, but that's far enough to forget, and the people in front would have to crane their necks way around to look at you, so you're safe that way. Maybe there's a lady in front of you chewing out her husband, or, if it's late at night, maybe he's trying to get his hand down her pants right on the bus, and you can see him trying to work it if you look between the two seats. That's what I saw on the way to Maine. When I saw it, something happened to me. You know the way the seats hum on the Greyhound: I could feel the humming up inside me, and everything ached. I felt like somebody was scooping out my insides and leaving a big empty hole. It was a good thing I was on a bus. If I wasn't, I could have done something crazy, *anything* to get rid of that feeling. I closed my eyes and remembered how Mike was. Whenever we went anywhere at night in his car, he had to stop somewhere and unbutton his jeans and ask me. On the bus, all night, I thought it would be worth it, for the company. But that was before.

)

The guy pushes his duffle under the seat with the toe of his boot and lowers himself in. The way he's built, you can see it hurts his body to sit down, because every muscle has to be in on it. Without moving my head I can see how every time he takes a breath, the curve of his blue jeans tightens a little more over his leg. I keep my eyes where it is smooth and flat, where he taps his fingers to the *tsch-tsch-tsch.*

I like to look at people's hands. I like his because they're tan and clean, the fingernails barely pink, like somebody blushing, trimmed and square across. You know those little white marks on the fingernails? Mom told me a rhyme when I was little: one mark means a gift, two a new beau. I forget exactly. His fingernails don't have any marks that I can see. Mine have one for a gift. I wonder if it's a gift I already have, or one I'm getting.

He shifts in his seat; people can feel it when you're thinking about their hands. They get more uncomfortable than if you look at their faces. Anyway I don't need to look at him. That's what it means to have Jesus inside you, the man said. So why did Jesus make this guy sit next to me, out of all those seats? The man in Maine would have said it was a test. *Are you strong in the ways of the Lord, or are you an open door for Satan?* But he didn't see this guy. One of his hands could curl around my leg and I wouldn't be able to get away. That's how skinny I am.

)

My hairbrush is jabbing me in the butt; I forgot I had it there. I guess I was going to brush my hair in the station, for my parents, but I forgot. Will it look weird if I do it now? Will he think it's a come-on? If I don't, it looks like I'm one of those girls who don't care, and my parents are going to pick me up in Willamantic, that's another reason. The man said if I was unsure about something, to ask Jesus and he would tell me what to do. It's for my parents, I tell Jesus. He says okay. It feels good. I like the pull on my scalp. I like seeing the pink handle come by again and again, and the smoothness of my hair. I brush it for five minutes, at least. Mom says it's not plain brown like some people's. It's got lights in it that people notice.

)

Tsch-tsch-tsch. He has to have it on pretty loud for me to hear it like that. Mom hates headphones. She said a kid got killed the other day riding his bike with them on. That driving beat, she said, makes us think we can walk in the street without looking; that we can walk all over this world without watching it. When I get in to Willamantic, she's going to say that's what got into me and why I took off. I don't know what got into me but it wasn't that. I was good. I called them from Maine when it was all over. I dialed the phone in the bus station, shivering so hard I had trouble hitting the right buttons, and had to start

over. I wish she'd seen me then. I called and said, "Mom, I'm
coming home. Jesus is my savior and I'm a new person now."

She said: "Just get on that bus, Jesus or no Jesus."

"I really am, Mom," I said.

"Did you hear me," she said. "We'll pick you up in Willamantic. Two-ten and don't pull any funny business."

When the bus pulls in she's going to see me sitting with
this guy and grill me. "Who's that?" she'll say. "Where do you
know him from?" If she sees me brushing my hair, she'll say:
"That's asking for it. You know that, don't you?"

❩

I put the brush in my purse. That's when he turns to me. His
hands rise up off his jeans and I can't help it; I shiver a little.
All he's doing is taking off his headphones: that's all. He lifts
them off and sets them in his lap, and they keep *tsch*-ing; he
has them on that loud. He lifts his hair out of his eyes, but it
falls back across again. I like his hair. It isn't dirty or messy.
It's like his hands: smooth and light brown. He's not much
older than me. I can tell that.

"Cold?" he asks. He looks right at me, first into my eyes.

I wish his eyes would stay there, but they don't. They
never do. They flick down a little, fast, and then come up
again. That's something I would change.

I touch the cross and his eyes flick again and this time
when they look back up they narrow and focus hard, just for
a second. If he asks me am I religious what do I say? What do
I say so he stops checking me out? He only does it for a second.
He has nice hair, nice hands. Maybe he would listen if I
phrased it right.

"So, what's your name?"

"Anna," I say. I don't want to. I want to give a new name. Laurie. Or Ellen. My name comes from the outside, like my voice. That's how fast I say it.

"Where you headed, Anna?"

"Willamantic."

"Willamantic," he says. "Me too. I'm going to Willamantic."

"I'm visiting friends."

"That's cool. I'm visiting friends too. These friends of mine have a dune buggy. Have you ever been on a dune buggy?"

"Sure," I say.

"Me and these friends, last time I was down, we turned it over on the beach. We drove it right into the water, didn't let up on the gas at all. We rolled it four times. We coulda died, it was that close. We coulda been smashed completely dead. What a rush." He brings his hand down hard on his leg. "Are these girlfriends or boyfriends?"

"Oh, girlfriends," I say. "We've had some crazy times together too." I wonder if he would listen if I told him what happened, not with my friends.

"Like what?" he asks.

"Like this one time we got drunk and blasted Prince on the radio and went into a spin on the interstate."

"Yeah," he says. "My friends and I do stuff like that, mostly on motorcycles. The thing that gets me: you can do the craziest thing and not get killed, and then you're just standing there one day and something happens."

"I know," I say.

"I had this one friend, Paul. He was a wild man, always taking off on his bike alone after parties, and driving off into the heaviest fog he could find. He *looked* for the heaviest fog, and nine times out of ten he was so drunk it didn't matter. One night he took a friend with him, and they were perfectly sober. The fog was bad; real yellow and low, the kind where you don't see headlights until they're two feet away. At one point this friend yells to Paul that he has to take a pee. Paul does too, so they pull their bikes off the road and the friend goes a little farther into the weeds. The fog is so heavy they can't see each other a few yards apart. The friend hears a car engine; sounds pretty far away, but that's the fog, too, and then this dull kind of thump. I guess Paul thought he was off the road and he wasn't. It really gets me. The man was taking a pee."

He's quiet a minute, sort of pushing his hands along his jeans and looking my direction, only out the window. I look out the window with him and after a while he leans back.

"That's pretty sad," I say. "I heard a story the other day. The girl didn't die, though."

"That's good," he says. His voice is hoarse. He doesn't ask. I know if I could tell it right, he would have to understand. He would have to be sick not to. I wait. After a minute he asks what happened.

"It was pretty strange," I say. When I begin, my voice is shaking, but he doesn't look like he notices. "This friend of mine took off for Maine. She didn't tell anybody where she was going. She left right from school and went up there: seventeen hours. She was in a coffee shop in this town, Stonington—"

"I know Stonington," he says.

"Yeah? And it's just her and this lobsterman and the waitress. She got a cup of coffee and was feeling pretty bad; she'd forgotten why she'd gone up there, and neither of these people would look at her. She said it was like she was invisible, and nobody on earth knew where she was."

"That's a bad feeling," he says.

"Only then this guy comes in and looks around and walks right up to her booth and sits down. And he says: 'You have not been baptized in the Lord.' 'Yes I have,' says the girl. 'When?' 'Like everybody else, when I was little.' 'That's not baptism,' he said. 'That's your folks.'

"He had these blue eyes. They were wide open, staring at her. He didn't blink at all; it was like he was awake all the time. He said: 'You're incredibly unhappy, little girl.' My friend said it was the 'little girl' that got her. Somebody used to call her that. It was like he knew it. Anyway, he made her nervous, so she crossed her arms and looked in her coffee cup. 'I'm fine,' she said. She didn't want to be rude.

"He reached across the table and touched her hand. 'No you're not,' he said. 'Why don't you cry, if that's what you want to do? You will baptize yourself in your own tears, Praise Jesus.' She said the way this guy said 'Praise Jesus' gave her the chills up her spine. Like he knew something she didn't.

"She didn't mean to, but she started shaking. She was pretty hungry and tired and it was like he knew her. He stood up. 'If you come with me,' he said, 'just down to the beach for a minute, your whole life will change.' She thought what the heck. Nobody looked up when they walked out together. Anybody in their right mind would've looked up, but not those folks.

"She followed him down the street to this cove, where a couple of dinghies were tied up to a pier. It was cold, about to storm. The water was dark gray, you know, like it is up there, and when she listened to it slap against the side of the pier, it made her feel worse. That's weird, isn't it?"

"Not too weird," he says.

"Anyway, the guy wades into the water. 'Come on,' he says to her. She said it would have looked dumb to have come that far and then run away, so she took off her shoes and socks and put them on the pier. The water was unbelievable. She didn't think she could stand it higher than her ankles, and there he was, in up to his waist, smiling at her and holding out one hand like he was having the greatest time of his life. She went a little farther, her legs going numb—and you know how it feels when your jeans are wet, they cling like they're alive or something. A wave came smacking up her legs, and when it touched, she wanted to cry, it was so cold."

"I can imagine," he says.

" 'Don't stop walking,' said the man. I think she felt the way you did with your friends when you were driving into the water in the dune buggy. Like there's no going back, you just have to take what's coming."

"For sure," he says. He shifts in his seat.

"This is taking too long, isn't it?"

"No," he says. "No. Go on."

"So the man put his hand on her head. 'You die in order to be reborn; there is no other way to do it. There is no other way to change your life.' "

"God," says the guy. "Did she really let him do this?"

"Wait," I say. "So she said, 'if you mean *really die* I'm

getting out.' He was still smiling, looking at her with those blue eyes.

" 'You have to go as far as you can in that direction,' he said. Then he put his hand on her arm in a nice way. 'Put your trust in the Lord and nothing bad will happen to you.'

" 'Okay,' she said.

" 'I'm going to hold you under a long time,' he said. 'When I let go, stay under *as long as you can*. You must choose to do this, or it won't work.' And his hand pressed on her head, pushing her under."

❯

I think about it a minute. I want to ask him: in the dune buggy, when you went under the waves and the water rushed in on all sides holding you under, what did you think about, before you started to fight to get up to the surface? Did you think, just for a second, "Who put me here? Why do they want me to die?"

❯

Aloud I say, "His hand was hard. She pushed, but his hand was stronger. She swallowed salt water; it went up her nose and mouth. She thought, no way is it supposed to be this bad, so she grabbed his arm and he let her up. She shot up so fast you wouldn't believe it. She said before she saw him she saw the sky, and this one gull standing on the pier about a foot from her face. She'd never seen one so close. It was pure white and clean and it just sat there taking it all in.

" 'You failed Jesus,' said the man. 'You must obey this time or all your life will be for nothing. I am only the instru-

ment of His pleasure. I do what He bids me, for your sake.'
He put his hand on her head and pressed down again. This
time she was ready, and got some air before she went down.
Under the water, she almost liked it. She thought, in a way she
would like to stay under a long time, it was so quiet and still.
Then she started thinking: when is he going to let go and let
me do this on my own? Because she was running out of breath
and his hand was still there. She opened her eyes. The salt
water stung but she looked around and his legs weren't there.
He wasn't there and something was still holding her down.
Bubbles flew up in front of her face . . . she must have said
something, but she doesn't know what. She reached up and
felt something hard and flat. She felt all along it, but there
wasn't an end. This is *it*, she thought. This is how I am going
to die, and no one will ever know."

"What happened?" says the guy.

"She found the edge," I say. "He'd walked her under the
pier, and the tide was in."

He doesn't say anything.

"I think he was sincere," I say. "Because when she got
back to her shoes and socks, there was a note, and a little cross.
It was pure silver."

"What did it say?"

"It said: 'And ye will know Satan, and come to recognize
his ways.' "

)

The guy is quiet and I am too. We sit that way a long time.
Then he looks at me. He says, "Have you got a boyfriend or
anything?"

"No," I say. "Why?"

"I don't know. You're just really pretty and I thought you would."

"Oh," I say.

"So how come you're so quiet all of a sudden?" His voice is nice. It's sweet and quiet. Mike used to be like that, sometimes.

"I was just thinking," I say. "Even if that guy wasn't sincere, it sort of makes me believe in the Lord."

"Oh," he says. He looks at my cross and then down at his lap. He holds up the headphones. "Dumb, huh?" he says. "These things were on the whole time we were talking."

"That's okay," I say.

"Ever listened on one of these?"

I have. Nights in a car, Mike would put the headphones over my ears. He would reach up my skirt and keep driving down the highway toward the falls. There weren't any lights on that road. He reached between my legs, then he'd push my head down toward his lap. His belt buckle was always cold against my fingers when I undid it; sometimes he pushed a little too hard and it hit my teeth, cold. It was quiet, only me and the road underneath, and in some ways I didn't mind. In some ways, it was all right.

"No," I say. "I never have."

"I can't believe it," he says. "You don't know what you're missing. The beat really gets me on these 'phones. I crank up the bass and really feel it in my gut, you know?"

I let him put the 'phones on my head, fix them so the two foam circles press against my ears. I feel them pressing, I feel the metal band around my skull. He looks at my face; first into my eyes, then down to my nose, my lips. Without meaning to, I have smiled and nodded: yes the volume is fine up that high. His eyes smile now; they no longer search my face, but look beyond me, a little unfocused, as if he forgot what he was looking at.

He's right. The beat is strong. It moves down through my arms and legs, it makes me heavy down there, where he will touch me if I let him. He watches my face as I say words. I say: *Tell me when we get to Willamantic. I don't want to miss my stop.* I know my lips move, but the music is so loud I can't tell whether my voice came out, or if I just mouthed the words.

A Daughter Who Sings

My biggest fear is that you won't believe me. My mother, who has a different angle on this story, says that a hundred years ago, when Maupassant was alive, there'd be no question. "For God's sake," she cries. "It's life; things *happen!*" Then, as if she's walked over some line I can't see, she leans back in her chair and shrugs. "So be my guest," she says. "Leave out the important part."

She's waiting, and it seems to me that houses by the ocean are the quietest in the world: you're listening so hard for the regular wash of the waves to keep going, up-and-back, up-and-back, that you accidentally hear how quiet the inside of a house is. I'm only visiting now, but the exaggerated quiet still bothers me, and it's what I don't understand about my father— why he moved us here, planted us on this cliff and said, "The gig's up for me." It's been a while since his memorial service, but I remember one of his stockbroker friends coming up to me. He stretched one arm toward the ocean view, just like

Father. "You'll hear it called a lot of things," he said. "Ambi-
tion, ants-in-the-pants, ghetto-fever. But the way I see it, your
dad was just looking for something big enough to match his
worries." Then the stockbroker folded his arms across his
chest and shook his head, though I hadn't said a word.

"You're a kid, for God's sake," he said. "Try to enjoy
your life."

If I could have answered the stockbroker, I wouldn't have
argued, exactly; I would have just asked what he meant by "big
enough" when Big Sandy was too big for me; why, when we
moved there, I was lonely in a new, shivery kind of way, the
way I imagine performers feel when they're caught out on
stage and haven't finished memorizing their part. Ours is the
last house above Big Sandy, and according to Father, we had
no choice but to build farther out; otherwise our view of the
Pacific would've been cut off. He managed to build so that the
ocean takes up your whole vision when you look out. This was
fine at what he called his "stage of life," but I had to lean
backwards out my bedroom window to catch a glimpse of our
nearest neighbors, the Walkers.

We came from inland like just about everyone else my
parents knew. Sometimes it looked like the entire congrega-
tion of Temple Judah was moving to the beach, but since each
family settled in a different town along the coast, we were back
where we started. Father was the only one to build on a cliff.
He built fast, as if any minute someone from the town associa-
tion might show up with an official piece of paper bearing our
name, and as a result, the house came out looking like an
unfinished ocean liner with all its portholes on one side. From
down below on Big Sandy, you could see people moving across

the living room, or coming out onto the deck to shade their eyes and search for you. I used to ask Father not to wave and point at me down there, but he said it was nothing to be ashamed of, to live in a beautiful place and have a few people accidentally notice.

At the time, this struck me as a new pinnacle of adult hypocrisy. What did he know about beautiful places? He didn't sail or swim or take advantage of the beach in any way. He hardly walked out into the fresh air, let alone went down on the sand. His leather recliner faced the television set, not the ocean, and early in the morning, when he watched the stock returns, the glare off the water was so strong he had to close the drapes in order to see the numbers. As far as I could see, his communion with nature consisted of bringing guests up to the picture windows, or driving down the coast with his hand out the car window, crying, "Look at this, would you?" I was sure Mother was as embarrassed by these displays as I was; she was always asking him to roll up his window, claiming she couldn't hear her Mozart.

So I took it as a sign of honesty that the Walkers never carried on about the view. Mother says it's because Mrs. Walker was an interior decorator. The minute our house was done, she and her husband dropped by to see what we'd done with the inside.

Mother was aghast. All our money had gone into the headland, she told them. It would be ages before we could redecorate. I'd never heard her talk that way, never heard a word like *decorate* out of her mouth. Inside, of course, our house was like our old one: our plaid davenport, Father's black recliner, and where else, Mother asked the Walkers, where else do you put your books and phonograph records? And that? Oh, that, she said, was her own mother's heirloom tea cart; the family joke was that she almost sank the steamship bringing it to the United States.

Mrs. Walker hadn't yet found a way to move into our living room. Darkly tanned and slender in a white caftan, she looked to me like a little girl dressed up in a sheet for Halloween. She bit her lip, and I saw that our dark furniture made her dress glow. Her husband strode easily into the center of the room, planted his feet firmly apart, and gripped Father's hand. Next to Father's legs, Mr. Walker's appeared powerful and flexed, ready at any minute to catapult him from our midst. He complimented Father on the design of the three narrow levels, and on the black iron ship's stair that led to the bottom floor. He said how thoughtful it was of my father to give me a secret den of my own. I waited for Father to admit that it was *his* secret den, but he only winked at me and said, "She couldn't stand us without it."

Mr. Walker smiled brightly at Father. "This is going to come out wrong, but I have always been a great fan of Jewish humor."

At this, Mrs. Walker seemed to come to life. "Our Alexis is a very private person herself," she said, taking tiny steps forward in her caftan. "She would have come with us today, but her choral group is rehearsing."

"Oh," said Mother. "A daughter who sings."

I knew better than to look at Mother when she said this. Her head would be tilted a little to one side—that's her attitude of attention, the one she has when we're listening to the radio and a piece she loves comes on. I knew at that moment her eyes were taking in every feature of Mrs. Walker's face, with a look of expectation I've never seen in anyone else. When I was young and told that I had an ear for music, she gazed at my teacher for a full minute in this way, as if he were revealing not some kid's slight gift, but a great truth, a sign of hope for the entire planet. I never got anywhere with music, but Mother is good about it. She never hounds me, never gives me a significant look when the subject comes up in company. Just then, I could have safely looked at her. Only much later would she say to me that whatever ability a person discovers he has, it costs something to follow up on it, and you can't say in advance what this cost is going to be. Her voice was quiet and ragged when she said it, as if it were bumping into something along the way. I looked down; I wasn't sure who she was thinking of.

❧

Alexis Walker wasn't home a few days later, when her parents invited us over to see the inside of their house. Here I should explain that Mother is one of those fragile-skinned redheads you never see blushing; in awkward situations all color simply drains from such a face. As we stepped over the threshold of the Walkers' house, Mother turned exactly the sand color of their living room, like one of those sea animals that knows how to camouflage itself in danger. The room resembled a beautiful, spare art gallery; it contained only a long, grainy-looking couch and chair, and a glass table filled up inside with exotic shells I could never find on Big Sandy. The only brilliant spot in the room was an enormous woven rug showing six sandpipers, each framed in a different background of coral, vermilion, pale blue. The birds, caught in their separate frames, looked slightly confused. My mother laughed, then put her hand up to her mouth.

"Jessica designed everything, right down to the sandpipers," said Mr. Walker. "The only thing she forgot was how white shows up the dirt. We try, Alex and I, we do, but we just can't stay clean!"

This was for our benefit; there was no dirt anywhere. Now Jessica Walker's white dress blended perfectly into the room, so that you couldn't help but notice her dark gold skin and the delicate chain roped around her ankle. Her skin was the warmest shade in the room, in the whole house, it turned out. We were escorted from room to room, from a big bedroom painted a pale, hazy blue, to a terra-cotta kitchen where Jessica Walker smiled and murmured to my mother, "sunsetty." The only colors missing in the house were those of the ocean as it was just then, a dark winter blue flecked with whitecaps that caught the sunlight and turned it harsh, so brilliant it hurt your eyes to look at it directly.

Mrs. Walker paused before a door, leaning her head against it and knocking softly. "I'm silly," she said. "I know for a fact she's not home."

The door opened onto a small private hallway, and a room and bathroom painted a startling white. The curtains and bedspreads were the bright, elementary yellow of a child's five-color paintbox.

"Cheerful, isn't it?" said Mrs. Walker. "I gave her a choice."

Mother nodded solemnly. "It's as a young girl's room should be." She glanced around the neat, bright room as if looking for something in particular. "Oh," she said at last, pointing to a doll on the bed. "A harlequin!"

Mrs. Walker peered into the room with Mother. "Oh," she said, "the clown doll. Isn't it sweet—it matched so perfectly, I couldn't resist."

Mother didn't seem to be listening. She was asking Mrs. Walker if Alexi knew Stravinsky's music for *Petrushka*, the harlequin figure was just like it.

"Mother," I whispered. "They sell them in department stores."

She shot me one of her famous expressions, the one in which she seems to be returning from some place I can't yet imagine, and in silence went back along the hall with Mrs. Walker, who hadn't known the answer to the Stravinsky question.

After they were gone I looked around the room myself, for some little thing that would tell me what a singer was like. It was the kind of room shown in magazines as an ideal one for the teenager, a room where a girl sat cross-legged in a terry-cloth robe with a phone tucked under her ear and chin. One side was a big sliding glass window looking out onto the ocean, another was a full-length sliding mirror closet, closed up tight. School books were stacked neatly on a desk and whatever little objects or tokens she must have had were hidden somewhere. The little harlequin lay limply on the bedspread, its tiny perfect porcelain face delicately touched with red for lips and cheeks; only the dark lashes indicated the sorrow Mother was thinking of when she cried out *"Petrushka"* like she was dying of thirst. Alexis had been given a choice, her mother said, and she had chosen a room in which she'd be catching herself all the time in a big mirror. Her mother or father would always be knocking at the door, saying, "Alex, whatever you're doing in there, why don't you come out and share it with us!" Maybe the blankness was on purpose, part of a singer's self-discipline, like saying, *nothing for me, thanks.* But just in case she was a little bit like me, I wondered which made her most nervous: herself in the mirror, her parents at the door, or the big windows through which you could imagine the whole world was watching, or nobody at all.

)

That was when I started leaning out my own corner window to catch a glimpse of her before school, expecting a tanned, blond copy of Jessica Walker with only an armload of sheet music to ruin her disguise. I was proud of my own realism, since I secretly hoped for a pale, brooding, dark-haired figure who would drift past on the headland never looking my way. There were few girls of this description in Big Sandy, even among the drama and music students, the ones known as "moles" and "geeks." Almost everyone lay on the beach during the summer months. From June to August the wide strip of Big Sandy was covered with barely moving bodies. We lay there perfectly still, which at first is not as easy as you think. You want to get up and run up the dirt path to your house and your bedroom, and close the curtains so that no one can see you. Then, after a while, you realize you're still lying there, and it's difficult to move at all, even to turn over. It was winter now, but I lay in my bed the same way, unable to move. Every morning Mother came to the door, pushed it open, and walked away without saying a word.

Alexi was always gone by the time I got up, and in our school, the music people hid themselves behind the arts building; you saw them clustered in their dark coats or, on concert days, in long blue robes—whatever they wore, they always seemed to be in costume. In any case, Alexi was two years ahead of me, and a music mole on top of that. I wasn't about to ask. I set my alarm clock earlier and earlier, until at last I was awakening to Father's heavy footsteps, and the voice of the stock market commentator saying what was up, what was down. It was just past dawn. Crouching on my bed and leaning out into the cool, salt-sticky air, I saw a dark-haired young woman, utterly grown-up in stockings, heels, a navy-blue skirt—she could have been one of my teachers—striding up the drive our houses shared. She was spectacular; she didn't fit at all in that bright, childish room, and I was so pleased with the vision that I did not realize at first she was waving, shouting to me.

"Hello in there," she cried out. "Are you on your way to practice?"

I couldn't speak; I shook my head violently to indicate my answer and hauled myself back inside, out of her line of vision, fast. After a moment had passed and I could be reasonably sure she'd moved on, I peeked out again, in time to see her reach the top of the headland. She walked with a strangely familiar, springy step, her feet slightly turned out like a marionette. It didn't suit her at all—it looked like a mockery of girlishness.

Now I began to see her in the school quadrangle, sometimes quite far from her corner of the arts building. I wanted her to stay there—she was wonderful from a distance, exactly as a singer should be; she had a face and eyes that would probably look overdone, suffocatingly big up close, while from, say, the back row of an opera house, the bright, confident smile and the arched eyebrows that appeared always raised, always about to lift her face into the upheaval of song, would be brought to scale, down to human proportions. She bore no resemblance to either her mother or her father; I relished it. This enabled me to fall into a vague and violent fantasy of European heritage and adoption, and a more violent (and inevitable) confrontation between Alexis and her parents, in which she would demand to know the true origin of her exotic name, then run off to change into the great foreign singer she was meant to be. My imagination was lazy; the only part of the fantasy it could grasp was the picture of a girl who looked nothing like Alexis splashing vile colors of paint on pure white walls, and cutting up a yellow bedspread with scissors. This picture made me shudder as if an emotion I hadn't known I had was coming unchained and rattling around in my chest.

One afternoon, when I got home from school, I heard women's voices downstairs in the kitchen—my mother's and one I didn't recognize. Immersed in my dark-spy world, I crept back outside, listening to the rise and fall of the new voice, not wanting to hear the exact words. After stopping a moment, the voice began again, alone, moving upward in a haunting spiral. There was so much strength in the voice that it was as if the singer believed an orchestra stood behind her, or *inside* her—and made you imagine the fullness of all those instruments too. When she stopped, my mother clapped loudly, and the sound of it was miserably singular, ever-diminishing. I was well hidden by the side of the house when I heard the two voices mingling again, coming nearer the door. My mother sighed once in response to something Alexis said. "You watch," my mother said. "You'll grow into yourself beautifully."

)

Alexis Walker decided to grow into herself where no one from Big Sandy could watch her. The next fall she went east, to a music school in Boston, leaving me with habits I liked to imagine were her own. I no longer slept late, but awoke at the slightest noise with a ticking, nervous beat lodged in my chest and throat. Upstairs, Father moved back and forth, getting a glass of water, making his toast, opening the big window behind his recliner to let in the chill, lonely breeze. The window always stuck a little at first—I heard him yank it free in a long trailing sound like a car passing down the street, or a wave receding.

Standing before a bathroom mirror, I tried breathing correctly, deeply, as singers do. I lay on the floor as an old music teacher had once shown me: how lying down you could draw a breath so fully you felt that the whole world was inside of you. Then you let it out, and the miracle was, when you thought you had nothing left inside, you let out a little more. Breathing was natural this way, my teacher had said—*babies* breathe from their diaphragms—and somewhere along the line we forget, and the breath starts coming from a tighter place, higher up. My idea of discipline extended to the one other area I believed available: a carelessness in dressing that went with my picture of life in the east. Mother frowned; she did not see the other girls wearing black and maroon together.

What fad was this, and who did I think I was going to impress? Nobody in Big Sandy, I wanted to say, imagining a new room for my neighbor, one with bare, polished wooden floors and a bay window overlooking not an ocean but a narrow city street, and across the street a cafeteria where she ate breakfast and drank coffee and was joined by mysterious *others*, people whose musical instruments lay invisible in black leather cases, at rest in dark red or green plush, where anyone might be capable of playing them.

That spring I squeezed past the mathematics requirement of the college entrance exams and managed to get into the state college farthest north in California, a place clogged with dark firs and mists and brooding arts majors. My parents did not press me for an explanation—only once did Mother stop what she was doing and turn to me before I was ready. "You couldn't go any farther, could you?" she cried. I mumbled something about the school's fine liberal arts program, thinking only about the close-set pines, the small cluster of buildings in the fog. By late spring we hardly spoke without quarreling, and now I think that Alexis was on our minds the whole time. The day we got a letter from her, the gap of months dropped away as if we'd been discussing her the minute before. Mother handed the letter to me; I handed it back. Her fingers shook a little—in expectation of great things, I was sure—yet as I watched her read, I felt a vague thrill of dismay, like the one I'd felt when I saw the bouncing, childish way my neighbor walked. Hand-drawn musical notes ran jauntily across the rim of the notepaper. Alexis's handwriting was ornately rounded. She had dotted the "i" of her name with a heart.

"Did she get some scholarship?" I asked, looking away.

"Scholarship?" murmured Mother. "No." Her voice wobbled as she tried to hand me the letter. "She'd love to hear from you," she said.

"Not me," I said. "It's you she wants to hear from. You're the one who heard her sing."

Mother didn't answer right away. Her lips were tightly pursed, and from the dim center of my fantasy I thought they curved slightly with the pleasure she couldn't suppress. *She* had been chosen.

"Don't make it worse," she said, leaving the perfectly scripted note in my hands.

)

Alexis was due home in June, and we were the only ones who knew she was coming back early. Without an explanation, she had asked her mother to find her a *low-key job*, and Mrs. Walker had—she would be a teller in the Spyglass Savings Bank, a place where customers helped themselves to gourmet coffee and lounged on circular sofas. She'd also made appointments for Alexis with the dentist, the gynecologist, and a therapist, because as far as she knew, Alexis had done nothing about her health all year, even in Boston, a city full of doctors. Mother was miserable, sworn to secrecy. "It doesn't feel like life," she said to me after Mrs. Walker left our house one day. "It feels like a bad play. It *shouldn't.*"

Alexis arrived beautifully, on a day of glittering bold light and the Santa Anas, those hot gusty winds that feel like they come from someplace too big, a place of endless expanse, so that everything gets away easily. She'd told no one she was coming, and so it happened that her parents were out, and her taxi pulled up to our house instead. She wore a satin turban and big hoop earrings, and the whole effect, with her dramatic brows and dark eyes, announced the triumphant and calculated return of the successful artist after a first season. I had been right—she was not meant for close-up viewing; her eyes were fierce, their gaze so direct I knew she would open her mouth to accuse me of something, and I backed a step away. She came out with a high, quick, breathless laugh.

"Can you believe it," she cried to us. "Nobody's home!" I opened the screen door and she moved gracefully past me into our house, where my mother stood, her arms open. I will never know exactly what passed between Mother and Alexis that afternoon, for in shame I ran down to the secret den for which Mr. Walker had praised my father, where I lay face-down on the daybed. How long Alexis stayed I don't know. There was a long silence, and afterwards I heard their footsteps walking lightly above, walking, it seemed to me, over the whole earth. After a while I could not tell which belonged to my mother, which to Alexis. Then I heard the sound of a car coming down the hill, and their footsteps moving toward the front door. Alexis's parents were home.

)

That is where I would stop, if I had a choice. That is the moment to hold before the chest, stately and calm and dramatic in a way that wasn't enough for Alexis. There was a kind of harmony for a moment; even from where I was, I recognized it. But there was something else there too; a widening circle of ripples going farther and farther out from the center where the moment sank, beautiful, slow, unseen. I would stop before you guess the word *cancer*. If I say "cancer," Alexis's funny walk and arched eyebrows, her sophisticated outfit and embarrassingly eager little cry, *are you going to practice?*, will all be buried under a heavy blanket I won't be able to lift off afterwards. I could say *cancer*, too, about Father, even though it was still a year away, and immediately you'd forget about the way he watched the stocks early in the morning when the offshore wind bears something lonely, empty, toward your house, or the way he joked about the low, persistent fever when he found out what it was about: *the low I'll take,* he said, *can you leave out the persistent?* If I were alone in this, I'd leave it all out, but Mother says that's because I'm young and don't see yet that *this* is the part that matters. I'd end it without you ever knowing why Alexis behaved the way she did for any reason other than the pain of coming home again to find everyone looking at her the same as when she left; everyone refusing to have a new reaction, of being either shocked or pleased; only able to reabsorb her into their lives quietly and comfortably, without rocking the boat. Cancer or not, Alexis wasn't going to let this happen. She was going to compose this part of her life as if it were an opera. The problem was that the only person on our block who loved opera was my mother.

During that summer Alexi didn't sing at all. She worked half-time at the savings bank, even when the young man arrived from the east and Mrs. Walker began to make plans for their wedding. On the invitation it said, in perfect calligraphy that made even my mother wince: Join Us in a Celebration of

Life. I went into the bank once, and the young man, whose name I have never been able to hold in my mind, was sitting rigidly on one of the circular sofas, watching his bride. He looked familiar to me in a way I couldn't place, with his delicate determined features and reddish hair; Mrs. Walker told us he was a true *wunderkind*, at twenty-three already an accomplished cellist and a medical student. He'd seen Alexis *like that*, said Mrs. Walker, letting her breath out fast: it was wonderful how much he loved her. It was true that he watched Alexis with unnerving attention from his position on the sofa. His eyes were bright and soft with the consciousness of bravery, with the dream of seizing life at a moment of true drama, riding somewhere no one else would follow.

When Alexis first arrived in the taxi she had looked that way too, but now she held bills in her hands as if they were ashes, things slipping and unreal, disappearing in her fingers. Only once in a while did she look toward her fiancé, and when she did, an irritated smile passed over her features. She wore on her fingers a series of the cheap little filigree rings young women tellers sometimes wear, and rubber bands around her wrist, and for a moment I thought the whole thing—her job, her little rings, even her calligraphy—was a mockery of Big Sandy nobody else could see. But as I watched her handle the dry bills, counting steadily under her breath, I saw her concentration. She looked like she was following a musical score note by note for the first time, and to miss one note would be to step off the edge of a cliff. When I left, the young man was still sitting on the sofa, his elegant feminine hands clasped over one knee. It seemed to me that Alexis would never stop counting.

❯

The wedding was held in August in a gray clapboard pavilion on the harbor that is supposed to resemble something on Cape Cod. It's a place with a capacity far exceeding the number of guests Alexis told us she wanted, but Mrs. Walker later added that her daughter never said precisely what she meant by "a small affair," and with Alexis, who was a precise young woman, this meant it was quite open to interpretation.

We were early; my father had a mortal terror of arriving late anywhere and missing something, and for once Mother did not try to hold him back. She herself had been ready since morning, though she struggled over what to wear. "It shouldn't be too bright, too cheerful," she said. "It would be like a slap in the face to her." At last she appeared, having lost the look of patient waiting I'd seen on her face the two times Alexis came to us. Her mouth was tight again, her whole face set as if she were readying herself not for a wedding but for an exodus. She found us a parking place, and once inside the pavilion, she made sure we stood in an obscure corner, and stopped my father from jingling his keys.

The room was set up exactly like the madrigal dinners Alexis had participated in during high school. I'd been to one or two of them, surprised each time by the medieval gloom they achieved, with the dais and the long candlelit table for the singers, and with the faces of the singers themselves, kids my own age who stood up in dark velvet dresses and tuxedos, the girls pale in the candlelight and the young men solemn, who seemed to have been waiting all this time for an opportunity to change who we thought they were. In the back, a few students might giggle: *they* knew these were still the moles and geeks who hid behind the humanities building.

Amidst the blue and white decor of the dinner tables (surely the doing of Jessica Walker) appeared the Walkers and the young man himself. Only Alexis was hidden, waiting in a back room for her entrance. The three of them stood by the tables murmuring greetings to each person who came up the gray, hollow-sounding stairs. Mother murmured to me that it looked like the set-up for the concert recitals of her youth.

She said we might as well find seats; it was easier to sit and feel awkward than stand up and listen to my father jingle his keys. Mrs. Walker came up to us and Mother later commented it was the first time we'd seen her in a color other than white. She wore pale yellow silk, awfully close to bridal white, someone behind us said.

When the music began, it seemed to come from beneath the pavilion, scattering people into their seats, sending even the Walkers quickly down the aisle to the head table. The music swelled from its hidden place: somewhere, where we couldn't see them, were singers—fifty, maybe a hundred. Guests craned their necks around, but no one appeared. The music swelled up, as if someone had released it and it was floating up to us untethered. The audience quieted, strained to recognize the bridal melody. I thought I knew what it was; it began so stately and dignified, then moved, before you knew it, into an upward spiral of dark minor chords, like the person who wrote it was ascending a staircase endlessly, and wasn't going to stop until he reached a tiny pinpoint peak from which he could survey us all. It was the music Alexis sang to my mother in return for her solitary applause. When I looked at

Mother, her face was stony white.

"Faure's *Requiem*," she whispered, her mouth splitting open like a wound. "It's the *Requiem*, and nobody here knows it."

There was a great rustling now, the sound was soft, endless, a paper house collapsing, as everyone turned to the back to see her. Someone whispered, "What a cute idea, instead of bridesmaids," as a figure in black and white, with a white-painted face and black cap, moved gracefully into view. Mother's head bent down as the harlequin walked up to the young man with reddish hair and delicate hands whose face, like her own, was drained of all its color.

The minister performed the ceremony hurriedly, rushing through the vows as if rushing to finish an uncomfortable dream. At the proper moment the clown held out her white-gloved hand and the young man was forced to peel it off in order to put the ring on her finger. He stuffed the glove quickly into his pocket, and all afternoon we saw it there, dangling out, a thin, cheap piece of cotton. During the kiss, I looked again at my mother. Her head was held high, her eyes focussed on a spot beyond the dais.

)

I don't know how anyone got to the reception line, how Alexis's parents got themselves to the place the caterer indicated. The harlequin was docile, well-mannered; she had the best posture of any of them as they stood lined up against the glass windows overlooking the water. Mr. Walker seemed to have consumed the physical health of his entire family: his face shone, his legs were planted apart in his good dark trousers.

Beside him, Jessica Walker's slender arms drifted out from her pale sleeves. If you looked at the line quickly, your first impression was that *she* was the bride, so fine and small-boned, about the same height and delicacy as the young man beside her, the young man who leaned slightly toward her, his body inclined at an angle away from the harlequin.

Alexis shook hands most vigorously of all—a recognizable, borrowed vigor—it took me a minute to recall her father's hearty handshake. She stood planted firmly, the way he did, her legs sturdier than her mother's, whose slim calves barely appeared beneath her gown. One glance at Alexis sent you straight back down the line to the others. She was too bright to look at, no one could look at her for more than an instant, and so people passed quickly on to the young man with neat hands, and the charming, youthful woman beside him. Alexis and her father anchored them, framed them, that was all.

By the time I had gathered my courage, the line had fragmented. Mr. Walker stood beside the refreshment table, and my own father was nowhere to be seen. Later, when it was time to go, we would find him outside on the pavilion deck, gazing out at the debris floating in the harbor, his hair ruffled up like a bird's. He had been ready to go for a long time.

Out on the dance floor the young cellist had taken the hand of the bride's mother. They glided onto the floor to scattered applause, and a ring of bystanders formed, making the cooing noises that had been stifled by Alexis's outfit. The two danced well together, and gradually Mr. Walker moved farther away from the dance floor, into a tight mass of men in dark suits. Soon the floor was crowded with dancers, but you always saw, somewhere near the center, the pale yellow gown and the boy's head now dropped in abandon on the woman's shoulder.

Mother sent me alone, although there was really no line now at all. I took deep breaths to stop my trembling as I approached the harlequin, but it was no use. She reached out with her pale hands and pulled me close, looking unblinkingly into my eyes until my tears welled up, and I knew my mascara ran down my cheeks in two points of black like the exaggerated ones of her mask, until I performed with feeling what she could now only do by design.

She let go of me with a sigh. "You still don't breathe right," she said. "It's got to come from farther down, in here." She pointed at her own abdomen, but as she pointed, her laughter tore out from high up in her chest.

Without meaning to, I had begun to move past her, and she, without meaning to either, held out her hand to the air.

The World Is Full of Virtuosos

Everyone said it was a gift, that he shouldn't disparage it, shouldn't smile with his mouth closed and shrug like that, at least not in front of other pianists. It was apparent in him from an early age: no matter how brilliant his interpretation, no matter how deeply into the music he dragged his audience, they had trouble afterwards remembering his name or what he looked like. They could not be bowled over by his personal style and made to stand up suddenly, their hands raised above their heads as they cried, *Oh, bravo! Bravo!*

He was meant to be an accompanist.

Maybe it was the way he sat on the bench, slightly hunched, a little too close to the keyboard to give us the satisfying distraction of watching a graceful masculine figure. Or was it his hands, also kept close to the keys, never rising and falling from the ecstatic heights of his fellow artists—unbelievable heights—to make audiences perspire secretly into their palms, straining to see over felt hats and precarious coiffures, forgetting the music altogether? This never happened to him. Under the influence of Schubert, Brahms, and Wolf he turned pale and ghostly, as they say great composers do in a crisis of inspiration. After a performance he rushed from the stage to the artists' room in such a manner that no one dared follow, leaving the singer alone on the platform with her roses, which was what everyone wanted anyway. But even when he was there, performing, it was difficult to see him, blocked as he was by the gesturing arm and torso of the singer upon whom all eyes were trained in the intimate salons and concert halls with maroon draperies, gold-tasseled ropes keeping everyone in the proper section.

The accompanist took solace in his invisibility. Unperceived by anyone, he left the guarded rooms altogether, descending into a long, narrow country whose delights and terrors he had known since childhood, and which passed beneath him like a film while he held still, keeping his balance. It was a country whose peasants were cunning (though foolishly dressed) and whose nobility, overly fond of heavy signet rings, were frequently driven mad by dark moods and unmentionable diseases. The country's weather had a pattern only he could predict: blazing heat interrupted by the sudden, violent squall, clouds rolling forward, massive and cinematic across vast plains. The landscape itself was northern and intemperate, gouged by fjords and barren for long stretches. Occasionally a solitary figure, a weak silhouette, appeared over a distant rise, growing taller and more solid until its shadow draped him like a shroud, whispering, "Your turn, your turn," as he worked to sustain his invisible grace—for someone had once said to him: *A long life will be yours, and a quiet, growing influence.*

Immortality, after a fashion, though you will never know it. Only after the figure passed did he hear a small, plaintive, animal noise and feel someone tugging at his trouser leg. There was someone with him: a child for whom he had to wait, and whom he had to steady against the unpredictable forces surrounding them.

Returning to the concert rooms, bringing himself and his singer up to the surface, he often succumbed to a deep, sudden unhappiness, for at such moments he could take one look at his singer's back and be overwhelmed by a swarm of small miseries not his own. The broad velvet expanse of the Yugoslavian contralto who believed in herself utterly, utterly, revealed a woman whose bras were hooked so clumsily no lover could ever undo them; the thin shoulder blades of the soprano told him she was the sort of girl doomed to stand paralyzed before shop clerks, inevitably choosing an overpriced satin blouse that would flutter when she sang, sending chills of distress up the necks of her listeners. And so, in this world too, the accompanist did his work: he bowed his head and absorbed the contralto's excess of clumsiness, the soprano's nervous chill. With his own steady insignificance he warmed their backs, their throats, their voices.

At the moment of their triumph, by way of reward, he saw again the face of the man who had convinced him early on that it would be the greater achievement, the ultimate expression of his devotion, to become a fine accompanist. Seated behind the singer, he saw again his teacher's broad, mild forehead, his hazel eyes, heavy-lidded as if at any moment he might descend into an unfathomable dream: the eyes of an Eastern monk or a diplomat who has served so long in a foreign nation that he has lost his desire to go home. And during his brief, modest bow, the accompanist felt again what this man had taught him to enjoy: the steadiness and quiet freedom of working unsuspected in the public view, submerged in the daily, secret progress from which performers, for a moment, escape.

This was the teacher who said to him, when he was in his early twenties, "My boy, the world is full of virtuosos. Does it really need another?" The teacher, saying this, put his hands into the pockets of his dark gray cardigan and smiled: the young student's face was not yet the face of an accompanist. It was narrow and restless with the desire to take this scholarship, win that competition. The boy was still trying to cultivate an eccentric look: a careless, romantic style of dress whose trademark was a big, badly ironed white shirt that hung loosely on his slim shoulders. For a time, this had an effect: the big shirt, his fine wrists, and the uncultivated ardor of his hands made young women in the audience privately tremble. He listened to no one, exulting in the fierceness of competitions and brief, explosive affairs. And so it took a long time for his teacher's words to reach him.

It was without transition, without fanfare, near the end of a war in which he did not fight, that his name appeared in tiny print beneath the name of a famous soprano, on the marquee of a European concert hall. Inside, he sat at the piano, his hair neatly trimmed, his suit pressed. Only his white shirt, if you looked closely, bore the slight bagginess of his earlier style. Maybe this was all it took: a trademark gone unnoticed on a single occasion, unnoticed only because the patrons had, during the war, lost their knack of observing the minutiae of personal style and sat stunned, like small children, their hands in their laps, waiting for the music with the same blank readiness with which they had waited in lines for bread, margarine, potatoes, and the last delicacies available.

They had wandered into the concert hall as if blind, ushered to their seats by boys in white gloves who now waited at the doors to usher them out again. They waited through the first measures of Schumann's "Du Bist wie eine Blume," through the accompanist's slow, golden chords, each joined to the next as if to say, with calm confidence, that a break between them would let in chaos, destruction. Yet the audience waited as if listening for something in particular, a code word only they would catch, until the voice of the singer emerged like a thin green stalk out of the earth and a small sigh shuddered through the room. The singer's voice was weak, rasping, on the verge of failure, but the faces of the listeners shone. The accompanist quieted his chords and the singer cupped her voice like a candle flame. *This* was what the audience wanted: the sound of a single human voice emerging from an impossible place.

A sign of the times, he thought, a temporary craving—after the war he would go back to solo performance, win a competition, spend a year somewhere remote developing a virtuoso's repertoire, all new pieces! But when the war was over, the demand for solo singers only heightened: in Paris, Vienna, Amsterdam, audiences wanted to hear a single voice rising, accompanied by a single piano, nothing more, no orchestra! He was wanted everywhere at once. He needed an agent, and a tailor willing to make, on the spot, a half-dozen dress suits of fine but unassuming cloth, white shirts, black bow ties, and a crimson cummerbund for the winter holiday performances. Everywhere singers and their managers pressed his hands and said in hushed tones, "Why is it that there are so few truly great accompanists in the world?" Each time they said it, he bowed his head in the gesture that would be recognized after his death as the essence of his style: the small, closed-mouth smile and the shrug that everyone misinterpreted as self-deprecating when it was, in fact, a secret humor. *No,* he was thinking. *The world is full of great accompanists, all trying to be something else.*

On the opening night of a new season, a diva, turning to acknowledge the accompanist, noticed for the first time a thin gold ring on his left hand. After the performance, hurrying back to the artists' room, she saw the woman he had chosen: a plain, heart-faced girl with short hair—the easily startled type, the diva guessed—and so naive that she had dared to wear dark, practical corduroy to a concert! Her left hand, with its own thin gold ring, rested easily on the accompanist's shoulder, giving her the poise and quiet power of a figure in an old portrait. Not until the last moment did she move aside, and even as the diva approached the accompanist, she felt the young woman's presence like a mirror, reflecting back to her the absurdity of her passionate embrace, the one usually reserved for "special friends" in front of the paparazzi. Later, of course, she left this out, telling her friends and colleagues only how slight, how barely visible the wife was. *She's not a singer,* she cried, *not an artist, you can be sure of it!*

All that season and the season after, great sopranos and coloraturas, Dame this and Dame that, awoke their husbands in the early morning hours with their cries, their startled, chilled hands aching with unfinished, unsuspected love for the accompanist. Alone at night, the Yugoslavian contralto shuddered with envy, imagining the accompanist's hands discovering the slender country of his wife's modest back. The nervous soprano wept, knowing as if it were her own the exquisite shiver of the wife's responding touch. Perhaps she came as close as anyone could to the truth: that on his journeys now the accompanist felt someone beside him—not a child, tugging, but someone with his own curiosity, holding still in wonder as plains, dark gorges, and cloud-shadow rolled forward to meet them.

His concerts began to sell out, and for the first time in the history of the profession, an accompanist's name was printed in large letters, side by side with that of the greatest English soprano of the day. Infuriated, she changed her program at the last moment to throw him off, but he knew and loved the piece she chose: *a Schubert, full of small beauties,* he later told his wife. The audience that night was filled with his singers, some of whose careers had long since collapsed, and who sent long, school-girlish notes to the artists' room ahead of time. Seated in the front rows and in the upper tiers, they awaited his entrance, their breathing shallow with desire and expectation of the look of greatness: would he seem tall, his hair unconventionally long and slightly tousled, with perhaps just a touch of gray at the temples?

Imagine their disappointment when he emerged, for only now, as his teacher had foreseen, did he look like an accompanist. His forehead was a bit broad; he came out onto the stage wearing his glasses, and his initial bow was modest, brief, already turned toward the singer's entrance. When the performance began, he disappeared so completely behind the singer that the audience could not see the new, grave youthfulness of his face; could not see that he now had the two qualities necessary for greatness: the modesty of a son, an apprentice always learning, always grateful to take a backseat to some famous master or other; and the resigned calm of a father, a master who has recently accepted the terrible fact of adulthood: that he can no longer call himself an apprentice.

New York, London, Paris, Vienna. Every evening he took his place behind a singer with a series of deliberate movements that eased stage fright in novices and established artists alike. There he remained hidden, disguised. From the distance of the dress circle the audience could now see only that he was balding, and that his face had a slightly yellow tint—or at least it seemed so, compared to the smooth olive skin of the astonishing young baritone who had recently appeared in Vienna—a phenomenon! they cried. And generous, too. Everyone saw the young man smile when he invited the accompanist to stand beside him at the end of the concert. Handsome and unhurried, he turned sideways and gestured so gracefully toward the accompanist that afterwards it was his gesture, and not the accompanist, that was recalled.

Sometimes, when the accompanist was tired, the long landscape of the music took on a new menace, though one not entirely alien to him. As when he was young, practicing at his family's upright parlor spinet, particular chords struggled for power over him. An ominous, broad-faced man in a parrot-yellow jacket rose up to shake a finger at him while someone else, dark, trembling, no more than a shadow, came to his aid, crying, *there, there.* She was slender, a fragile thread belaying him to safety, telling him not to look down at the gaping dark canyon when that was all he wanted: to look, to see it directly. Re-emerging into the stagelight, he was weak, exhausted; her consoling cries hung in the air even after his part was finished. Behind the piano he heard, faintly, the broad-faced man's laughter, and he felt the edge of the dark canyon rushing to follow him up into the world.

By now, his name appeared on more record jackets than any solo pianist. Young accompanists—even gifted soloists—came to study with him. A school was founded in his name, and he was asked to write a book on the art of accompaniment, and to edit a new series: *Art-songs of the 20th Century*. New courses emerged, and his name was invoked by the world's great artists; it was said that he had transformed accompaniment into an art, an esteemed profession. Yet after concerts, he did not allow his photograph to be taken. He left parties early, missing the moment at which he might have told a famous anecdote or played alone before a private audience that would later make a legend, a myth, of his talent.

In the classroom, the accompanist put his hands in the pockets of his dark gray cardigan and listened, his eyelids heavy as those of a priest or seer, so that his students worried he might go into a trance and forget them altogether. He did not forget them. He told them how to anticipate and suggest a change in mood, when to fall back, nearly indiscernible, when to take command and become the voice: *here*, he said, *it is as if the singer's heart is too full to continue, and the pianist must take over*. And when the class was over, he sat with the one student still remaining, the two of them resting in metal chairs at some distance from the piano. He would look at the student—a boy or a girl a little tremulous and pale, who seemed to be fighting for air—and to this youth he would repeat the words of his own teacher, words so true they could only be recognized years later: "The world is full of virtuosos. Does it really need another?" He waited, then, for the bowing of the head that suggested—not just yet, but someday—submission to the mysteries of the quiet art.

A long life, and a quiet, growing influence: immortality after a fashion, though he would never know it. One day his picture appeared on the front pages of city papers in Europe and America. It was a kind, serious face that looked, people said, less like a musician's face than that of a prosperous merchant with a tendency to give credit during hard times. It was a photograph his publicity agent had suffered over, for despite all the sessions, weeks before his death, the photographer could not get him to look troubled or moody or shadowed by genius. Still, the photograph and a press release had gone out after his death, leaving the hands of the publicist with the scent of resignation on them—no one will pick these up, no one—and then, somehow, the story began to appear everywhere. A special was planned by a public television station, and newspapers sent their feature reporters and critics to the accompanist's lovely house in the countryside.

One Sunday, as families drove in and out of the cities, they heard on their car radios a low, charming, articulate voice: a woman speaking about her late husband's career. Behind her voice, a bright thrumming steadily increased—*redwinged blackbirds, cardinals, grackles,* she told the interviewer, laughing; *they love it here*—and the radio audience imagined thousands of birds, darkly clustered and hidden at the borders of a great lawn. Then the voices of the great singers were heard, singers whose backs the accompanist had observed over the years, divining sad, secret truths. And these singers, as they were asked to comment on the master's life, were drawn again and again to refer to themselves: what a great teacher he had been for them, how he had made them feel like artists from the first moment they walked into his studio as trembling beginners, how he made them hear their own voices for the first time. A great honor, said the baritone (his voice still youthful, he did not seem to have aged at all!), a great honor to have worked with an artist who never obtruded, never made himself *felt*, you know, in that terrible way that solo pianists do.

To close the report, the baritone is asked to play a recording of his last performance with the accompanist. For a moment there is silence, and then the sound of the piano: the incredible surety of the touch, the controlled blaze of deep major chords that suggests a landscape of sunlight on checkered fields and high, dramatic clouds moving slowly across the surface of the earth. In the eighth measure, the singer's voice emerges and begins to grow, taking its nourishment from an unreachable place. From this place the voice grows and rises up. It is the flame of a candle that can never be seen, and the audience cannot resist: they are drawn, they must listen, to the voice.

A Night of Music

Uncle Maury, my father's younger and only brother, used to say it was pure accident my mother married Dad and not him. "Women marry the wrong men all the time in great literature," he said. "Read Chekhov. Read Tolstoy." He made this statement in our living room the summer I was nine, pointing his glass of fiery bourbon at my father, who was resting on the sofa.

"Never hit a man when he's down," Dad said.

"You're not down," Uncle Maury replied. "You'll live to be a hundred."

He kept talking, and everything he said sounded not only like indisputable fact, but like a clue to an even bigger fact. I began to think that a story could never really be finished, and that our house could never be quiet in the way it is just after visitors have left it.

At the time we were living five blocks from the Pacific Ocean in a house shaped like a shoebox. It was set back from the street and surrounded by tall, slender eucalyptuses that were continually losing their leaves and acorns. The lot, with its trees and tennis court, swamped the little house. My father, who respected health, said it had been built by a former Olympic athlete who spent most of his time out-of-doors. My mother said no: it was a man whose dreams had overwhelmed his checking account. Uncle Maury, who came down almost every weekend from his studio apartment in Hollywood, was the only one who bothered to elaborate.

"Your family," he said, sweeping the air with his hand, "is living in servants' quarters. A great house once stood on these grounds. There were parties all the time, and none of them were masquerades for the Jewish Charity Fund. Elegant women swam in the ocean in their best gowns, and fascinating conversations went on all night. It is one of the tragedies of our era that the art of conversation is dead, and why, in all probability, we are lost." His glasses flashed as he gazed up into the tall, drooping eucalyptus, whose leaves pointed back down at him like skinny fingers. "I tell you, Rachel, whoever built this place had the vision of a Gatsby, in an era that could not support such generosity." Above him, the eucalyptus swayed and groaned, making uneven shadows on the lawn and saying something just as grand and indecipherable.

)

My father's illness had begun that spring. By this time he was in his fifties and had survived a list of prestigious diseases that I could recite at school when we were asked what our parents did. Polio, age four; scarlet fever, age seven; pneumonia as an army doctor in Texas, where he had to stay when his brother went on to serve as a doctor in Europe; and just last year, kidney stones. My list proved that I knew him as well as my classmates knew their fathers, despite his monumental age. Now I bragged that he had a slight fever, and it didn't have a name yet. If he took it easy, we could still have the masquerade parties, and Uncle Maury could still come down on weekends. I did not add that my mother was not keen on Maury's visits. She was worried about resistance.

Shortly after school let out for summer, Uncle Maury called, as my mother had requested he do before coming down. I answered the phone.

"Did you feel it?" he said. "Four point three on the Richter scale. My place is made of balsa wood; tell your mother I really don't have anywhere else to go."

Dad wasn't surprised that we hadn't felt the earthquake. "Fine," he said. "It will be good for Rachel."

"I fail to see—" said my mother.

"He can help with the next party," my father said.

"Help do what?" cried my mother. But it was too late.

Uncle Maury arrived while Dad was out for his afternoon walk. He came up our driveway with two suitcases, and from a distance, it was only the suitcases that gave him away. He had my father's bald, yellowish forehead and wire-rimmed glasses; he even wore the same kind of red golf cardigan. It was only when he came closer that I could see the tight set of his mouth, and the way he strode forward without limping. At the front door he explained that he had parked his Thunderbird around the corner.

"I don't want to look out the window every day and see it there," he said.

He opened the suitcases in my room. One was full of
tennis clothes and the other was full of books.

"I saved Dostoyevsky," he said. "You should see
the mess!"

I had never seen his apartment. "He doesn't need to live
in a slum," my mother often said. "He's a professional, for
God's sake." I pictured his apartment to be on the top floor of
a Hollywood Boulevard building, where red and blue and hot
pink neon flashed all night, and where, since the earthquake,
huge spidery cracks would divide the plaster, and the neon
would shine on piles of ruined books.

"Where's your *pater?*" he asked.

"He's getting his resistance," I said.

"Where's our favorite musician?"

"In the kitchen."

"*Mais oui,*" he said, holding out his hand. "Just let me tell
you this, Rachel. Never marry out of pity. Great women do
it all the time."

)

That summer, if she wasn't practicing the piano, I could hear,
from my room, the steady, accountable scrape of my mother's
vegetable brush. As we came into the kitchen, she took a carrot
from the drainboard, washed and scraped it over the sink, and
slapped it unforgivingly down on the counter. We watched
her for a minute, then Uncle Maury walked up and put his
arm around her waist.

"*Je t'aime,*" he said.

"What's that?" I asked.

"That's French," said my mother. She turned around, her

face warmly pink and blank. "Maury, did Rachel let you in?" She smoothed back a dark curl that had fallen over her cheek.

"Don't," he said. "It looks nice a little messy."

She tucked the curl behind her ear. "Abe should be home any minute," she said. "He says you saw someone about the tinnitus."

"It's slander," he said. "He feels guilty because he stole all the drama. Have they said anything about the remission? How long it can last, what his chances—"

"Rachel, why don't you and Maury set the table," she said.

"I'm an idiot, of course," he said. "I've always been an idiot—"

"Maurice, welcome to family life." Dad leaned against the doorframe, his hands in his pants pockets and his lips parted, suggesting he'd been there for hours.

Uncle Maury cleared his throat. "I was just telling your wife that if you ever mistreat her, she and Rachel are welcome to move in with me."

"You and the cockroaches and the prostitutes," said Dad.

"Is a prostitute where you get V.D.?" I asked.

"Where did you hear that?" cried my mother. "Abe—"

"What I need is a little nap before dinner," said Dad. "Maury, can you hold down the fort?"

"No," said my mother. "Abe, come back."

He was already gone. His left ankle, weak from the polio, clicked all the way down the hall.

)

All July Uncle Maury and I swam and played tennis. He told me what books I should read when I grew up, and what college courses would be a waste of my time. He told me how, when they were boys, the neighborhood bully had called my father a Cripple-Jew, and Dad had bloodied the son of a bitch's nose. "Your father," he said, "is a hidden genius. Someday he's going to surprise you." He said my father had made his way up from the ghetto to medical school, dragging Maury, an English major, with him. "You can't raise a family on a writer's income," Dad had told him. "Get yourself a good profession. Don't be afraid of success." Maury, on his part, tried to find nice dates for my father. He even sacrificed a talented young music major he'd had a crush on all year.

"Why in God's name did I do that?" he said. "Do you realize that but for that, and World War II, you could have been my little girl?"

I didn't understand.

"Never mind," he said. "I'll tell you when you're older. For now, just remember who wrote the Great American Novel."

"Melville," I said.

"You're learning," he said. "You're learning."

Sometimes when we came indoors my father was stretched out on the couch, his eyelids barely closed and his bathrobe tipping open over his stomach and chest. He didn't wake up when Maury bent over him to tie the sash. "Your father is descended from the Huns, who swept across Europe long ago," Uncle Maury whispered. I looked at my father's full, slightly moving lips; at the thin left leg crossed over the healthy one for all to see. I had the feeling that he was not really asleep. At any moment he would get up and announce that he had heard everything we had said about him, and then he would take my hand. "Now, Rachel," he would say. "Now I will tell you everything. What do you want to know?"

Meanwhile, it was only Uncle Maury who gave things away. Once he went back to Hollywood and returned with a tiny brown leather book.

"The Yale *Hamlet,*" he said in a hushed voice. "You won't find many of these around."

The book smelled wonderful—old and dark and permanent.

"Someday you'll look at this and remember your old Maury," he said.

"How old are you, Uncle Maury?" I asked.

"Only ninety-nine," he said, frowning. "And your father and I are both planning on being around a lot longer, so don't get any ideas."

In August my father asked Uncle Maury if he would honor us by choosing the next Jewish Charity Fund masquerade theme. Every evening for a week Maury leaned against the kitchen counter, a drink in his hand, arguing with my father. The suspense was unbearable. I loved the one hundred turquoise paper lanterns strung in the trees and over the tennis court; the immense and threatening net of extension cords that threaded across the edge of the court. I was allowed to stay up late and walk among giant Cleopatras and Neros come to life for one night only; powdered bosoms bent down to smother me and bright, chill jewels dented my cheeks. Uncle Maury was my favorite person at these affairs. Second-rate as he must have thought them, he had never missed one, and his costumes were always better than anyone else's. To the last party he had come as a fifteenth-century monarch who predicted the end of the world for 1965. Everyone else was "Age of Reason." He stood next to the refreshment table in a woolen robe, a silver foil crown on his head. Holding his drink at an angle, he pointed toward the ocean.

"They're being tested right out there," he said. "Someday, one is going to explode right next to the lighthouse, and then where will we be?" He glanced around at the other guests. "You and I are the only ones who give a goddam," he whispered. "Nobody else is willing to admit what's right under the surface."

The morning after that party, the ocean was darker blue and more mysterious than ever. The waves heaved themselves onto the beach as if they were tired of hiding whatever was underneath them, and I didn't want to turn away, for certainly it would happen when nobody was paying attention. Later that morning, as I hunted the chinks in the tennis court for dimes that had jingled out of people's pockets, I found, in the dank, evil-smelling hedge of the court, a clue to our destiny: a small empty box upon which a man and a woman embraced before a fireball sun, the ocean ablaze behind them. The woman had dark hair and resembled my mother. All day I played that the box contained a special medicine by which she would save Dad, Uncle Maury, and myself when the ocean let go.

Now, every evening, while my mother worked at the sink, Maury and Dad gazed abstractedly at the place where her white shirt touched her shoulder blades.

"Great literary lovers," Uncle Maury suggested.

"Fine, Maurice, whatever you want."

"You're not enthusiastic. You're never enthusiastic."

"This isn't the White House Ball," said my father. "Just decide."

"Let me ask you this," Uncle Maury said. "Are you going to be well enough to host, or do you want me to—"

"Go ahead," said Dad, sighing. "You're the host."

Finally Uncle Maury decided on the title: "A Night of Music." My mother blushed as she did the dishes. She was the only musician in our family. When she sat down to play, her face grew foreign and serious; you noticed her high cheekbones and her green cat's eyes, and she was nobody's mother. Uncle Maury made a stipulation. She had to come as Clara Schumann, charming wife of Robert Schumann, and a great pianist in her own right. Clara's career had gone down the drain, Maury said, because Schumann was a crazy genius and also gave her six children.

"Why Clara?" asked my mother, turning to him. "Why can't I be whoever I want?" She tapped her fingers on the counter and looked at my father. "Someday I hope to understand why everything is such a production with you two."

The afternoon of the party, Uncle Maury disappeared for three hours. At five o'clock, during my father's exercise time, I thought I saw Dad coming down the sidewalk, a tattered grocery bag in his arms.

"Dad," I shouted, coming out onto the sidewalk.

"An easy mistake," said Uncle Maury, smiling briefly. "It's been made before."

"What's in the bag?" I asked, looking down.

He held it forth; it had an acrid and sinister odor.

"Mothballs," he said.

In its depths I made out a chestnut-colored wig and the

gleam of a silver buckle amongst black cloth. "Are you going to be a witch?" I asked.

"Obviously you have been deprived of an education," he said. "Is your father home?"

"I don't think so."

"Shall we go keep your mother company?"

"Abe," said my mother, not turning from the stove as we came in. "If you're not feeling well, we'll simply cancel." Her voice was tender, solicitous.

Uncle Maury smiled the tight, brief smile again. "Before I die," he said, "I would like to see you as you were meant to be seen, in a strapless black evening gown, seated at a Steinway concert grand, playing the first notes of Schumann's great *A Minor*—"

"Maury," said my mother, still not turning. "I wondered if you would help Rachel with her costume. It's a little complicated."

"In a minute, in a minute," he said. He went to the kitchen cabinet and poured himself a drink. His mouth was set in a line, fixed on either side by a short, deep crease. His glasses flashed as he glanced up at the ceiling and down again at my mother. "Actually, I'm thinking of giving up that dump while there's still time. Move somewhere nice, like the beach. What do you think?"

"I think," said my mother, "that you enjoy creating dire situations, and that you'll never move. You enjoy the punishment."

"Ah, punishment," said Uncle Maury, taking a sip of his drink. "I like that. It shows you still see the romance in life's little situations." He leaned against the counter, and his mouth relaxed. "You know, Ruth," he said, "there's a crack all the way across my bedroom wall. I think it's structural."

"Move in here," I said.

"Rachel," said my mother. "Please don't say what you don't know." She wiped her hands on a towel. "Maury, when you reach a decision, please let us know. In the meantime, I am going to get dressed and so is Rachel. She has to get taped up."

"What about me?" Maury asked.

"You?" said my mother. We were halfway down the hall. She brought her hand to her mouth. "For Abe's sake."

At dusk the one hundred turquoise lanterns were switched on. They hung over the tennis court and in the trees like stars that have come out too low, revealing how fragile, how thinly glassed they really are. In my room, my mother wound black construction paper over my pajamas and taped the ends together. "Hold still," she said. "Now turn." I felt solemn and necessary, the mascot of her event.

"Eighth notes are quick and light and joyful," she said. Her face was pale.

"Stay in here," I said.

"I would," she answered, "but I have to get dressed too. Will you do me a big favor and keep Maury company?"

"Is he really going to die?" I asked.

"Where did you get that?"

"Did something happen to him?"

"No," she said. "It's just a ringing in his ears." She straightened up. "When you're older, I promise you'll understand. For now, will you just keep him company?"

I stood in my room a long time after she had gone. I did

not want to go find him; he would not be my Uncle Maury. Looking down, I saw the long black paper stem and bowl of the note, and over my head, a stiff black flag. If I moved too quickly, the sides of the stem bit into my arms. If I squatted, the bowl of the note folded into my ribs. It was possible that no one would recognize me. Terribly far away, my father's electric shaver roared. My mother opened jars and closed them, turned faucets on and off. Walking at last toward the kitchen, I heard the quiet chink of ice hitting glass.

Uncle Maury stood against the counter, exactly where we had left him. He had changed out of recognition. He wore immensely long, pointy black shoes and black trousers, a long black tailcoat and a vest that shone in some places. A black tie was wound around his neck so that his white collar stood high above it, hiding his jaw. Then I saw his hair. Where before there had been a broad expanse of forehead with a light fringe combed backward, there was now a sleek mass of dark hair, so much of it that there was no part. He took off his glasses, and beneath the mass of hair, in the dim light, his face had a chalky, disembodied glow.

"Hi," I said.

He lifted his face peacefully. "Hello," he said. He seemed to rouse out of sleep. "How would you like to be, just for tonight, my little girl? The daughter of Robert Schumann, brilliant, doomed composer."

"Mom wants me to be an eighth note," I said.

"And who do you think she is going to be when she marches out of that bathroom, Miss Eighth Note?"

"Clara Somebody," I said.

"Clara Schumann," he said. "Now, let us go forth and

survey your estate, my child. And I'll tell you a story about Robert and Clara, your parents."

Out on the lawn, ladies from the temple had set up a refreshment stand. As we approached, one of them smiled at Uncle Maury and poured him a drink.

"Adorable," another one said to me. "Ginger ale?"

Uncle Maury was already strolling away.

"Your father, Robert Schumann, was in love with the beautiful and talented Clara Wieck," he was saying. "But Clara's father saw that Schumann was deep down crazy, unfit for his daughter, and besides, she was too talented—and I quote—'to wind up with a perambulator.' "

"What's that?" I asked.

"Baby buggy," he said. "The young people were madly in love, but forbidden to see one another by the old buzzard, Papa Wieck. So one night, at a public concert, Clara performed three studies Schumann had dedicated to her the year before. He was in the audience, and this was her signal to him that she was ready to defy convention."

Apparitions began to appear under the eucalyptus trees; men in britches and white wigs; women in red gypsy dresses, holding guitars. Uncle Maury waved his glass at them and led me back to the refreshment stand. He refilled the glass and began to move it in slow, meditative circles.

"Did they get married?" I asked.

"Abe!" someone shouted. A man in a French beret, dark turtleneck, and ink goatee swung up to us and clapped Uncle Maury hard on the back. He turned.

"Oh," said the man. "I thought you were our host."

"I am," said Uncle Maury. "Temporarily."

The man stood beside us, nodding as Uncle Maury swirled his glass in tighter and tighter circles. "Well," said the man. "Great costume." He walked away.

"See, Rachel, the thing is this." Uncle Maury's voice came down from the moon, distant and thin. The lawn was filling up with strangers. I turned toward our house and the top of the note bit into my neck. The light was on in my parents' bedroom.

"Uncle Maury," I said. "First can we go find out—"

"Let me explain," he said. "It was like there were two Schumanns. One was the artist, the genius. Passionate, lunatic, absolutely unfit for this crude world. He is the one who gave us the *Concerto in A Minor,* the likes of which will never be created on this planet again. The other Schumann was a family man who wanted nothing more than to have his wife and kids with him, and to maintain even keel until he died."

He gripped my hand.

"Of course it was inevitable," he said, looking into the sky. "That one should drag the other into the grave after him."

I yanked on his hand. The bedroom light was off; our house had become a small dim box among the trees. My heart beat wildly; his wig hung farther over one side of his face than the other.

"To answer your question," he said, "they married. That first year was a dream. He composed hundreds of songs, the *Kinderszenen,* the great, maniacal *Kreisleriana.*

"And then he heard it for the first time. He was coming home in his carriage late at night and suddenly, when he should have been hearing only carriage wheels on a muddy road, he heard a chorus of trumpets all around him. Of course it was a medical phenomenon, a warning of his nervous illness, but at the time, he could not know. It was music—celestial, triumphant—unlike any he had ever heard. He must have thought, my God, if I could only write that down. And then, Rachel, the trumpets began to sound like something else. Without warning, a dirge, somebody's funeral march."

Suddenly a hand slipped around my arm. I began to cry.

"Maury," said my mother. "What are you telling her now?" She knelt in the grass. Her black velvet gown spread all around her, and her long, pale arms emerged out of the sleeves of a long cape. She had put her hair up; dainty curls slipped down her neck.

"Great Christ," said Uncle Maury.

"Hush," said my mother, but her eyes sparkled, wide open, as if she'd surprised herself. Her fingers trembled as she adjusted the flag over my head. "Rachel," she said. "Some people want to admire your costume before it gets knocked all to pieces."

"Should I have been Robert Schumann's daughter?" I asked.

"No," she said, looking up at Uncle Maury. "You were meant to be exactly who you are."

At that moment a man came up behind her. He was wearing all black, like Uncle Maury, with the tie wrapped around his high collar and a dark wig covering his ears. "Nice costume, Maurice," he said. "Who are you supposed to be? Haydn? Mozart?"

"Ask your wife," said Uncle Maury, readjusting the wig. "I have a date at the refreshment stand." He stalked away, his long shoes sinking into the grass.

"Is this a private joke?" asked Dad. "Something that maybe goes back before my time?" He had turned toward my mother, and his face was the face of an utter stranger. I thought of everything Uncle Maury had said, of the trumpets in the road, and the two Schumanns falling into a grave . . .

"Dad," I said. "Is anybody going to die?"

"Where did you get that?" he shouted down at me.

"Nowhere," I said. "Uncle Maury was just saying—"

He towered. "Don't you know not to listen to your Uncle Maury? He's been a goddam liar all his life. It's no wonder he can't get anyone—"

"Stop," cried my mother, catching his arm. She rose to her full height and let go of him. "Frankly," she said, "I don't care which one of you is Robert Schumann. I would just like someone to be social. Rachel and I are going now. If you want to come with us, please feel free."

As we walked toward a group of people waving and smiling at her, she turned once. He was still standing there, shifting onto his good leg.

"You asked for it," she said, to no one in particular.

❫

In my room she knelt and began to tug at the masking tape of my costume. It was nearly midnight.

"I want to leave it on," I said.

"Rachel," she said. "Don't give me grief."

"I'm not. I'll take it off in a minute."

She threw up her hands. "Between the three of you a person could lose her mind." She walked out, forgetting to kiss me goodnight.

Over the windowsill, guitars thrummed. Laughter, near-familiar voices passed close to the house; figures lurched across the yard holding shoes and wigs in their hands. I waited for her to walk by. I made deals with myself. If she came by alone, I would take off the costume and go to bed. If only Uncle Maury or Dad came by, I would go to bed, but keep the costume on until I heard her voice. I made up combination after combination, leaving out those that made me nervous. I don't know how much later it was that the two people ran across the grass in front of my window. The woman made a sharp sound—a laugh or a cry I couldn't tell—and out of the mix of instruments and voices, I heard my name. It hung in the air alone, luminous as a pedaled note. Your own name, called in the dark, has an urgency, as if the syllables themselves know that you might sleep and miss hearing them altogether. I heard *Rachel* in my mother's voice. Then all other voices murmured at once: a shawl of sound hung over our house to hide her.

Our front yard had become enormous in the dark. It was strewn with tall wobbling figures that did not bend down as I moved carefully past. She was not in the front yard; not in the street where a treasure hunt was being conducted; not under the eucalyptus trees where two men fought with swords. I edged closer to them, unable for the moment to remember how anyone looked in real life. The blue-lit trees were giant undersea bushes, their lanterns exotic, dangling fish. I headed toward the tennis courts, whose edges were a tangled net of extension cords, and whose hundred lanterns sparkled like phosphorus.

I found them at the far end of the court. My mother's

gown swooped about her. A curved slice of blue lantern light fell on her arm and on the side of her face, leaving to darkness the features of the man who stood just beside her. They stood near the hedge where, earlier that summer, I found the little box with the picture on it. The man planted his feet wide apart and began to pull her toward the hedge, whose alien odor I imagined I could smell from where I stood. When she did not move, he began to wave his arms violently about, conducting an enormous orchestra for her benefit alone. His wig was askew, and he did not limp, but what happened next was worse. He leaned toward her with an authority I had never seen in my father, and the wig slipped from his head. I waited for my mother to laugh and toss off one of her famous remarks. She did not. She bent in her velvet gown and lifted the wig. She lifted it up and bestowed it on his head, and as if by signal, he began to lean again, so precariously that I knew our world was going to end.

In my hand the extension cord had a snaky life of its own, and so did the crackling that went on and on around me as I brought down the whole delicate structure of lights. I gave a single screech and sat down recklessly among the bits of blue paper and glass. I heard the sound of feet running toward me from all directions.

"Who is it? Are you hurt?" cried my mother. "Abe, for God's sake, we need a flashlight."

"Where in hell would I find a flashlight?" shouted my father.

I considered his voice coming out of the dark. Pain came by like a parade.

"Daddy?" I whispered. "Is that you?"

"Sure, it's me," he said, with a certain awe. "You were expecting the King of Siam?"

❭

Uncle Maury could not have been far away, for he was the one who found the main tennis court switch and engulfed us in light. As he came up, guests gathered around, looking in with the white and sleepy faces of people at a zoo. My father took Uncle Maury's arm, grinning at me as if I were a photographer and he had at last found a pose he liked. Under the bright lights I saw moisture beading up on his forehead. Uncle Maury didn't look well either, but with him it was different. Beneath the false hair, his face had taken on the waxy shine of a cut gardenia, and he was cupping his hand to his ear. They made an uncanny pair, standing behind my mother in their pointed shoes, their black coats, their loosened wigs. It is a picture I cannot forget. Even now, after everything he told me has come true, I can only guess at the music he was hearing that night when my mother, my father, and I heard only the sound of the sea.